Ally Malcom, Accidental Sleuth

TWO SIDES
of the
MIRROR

E. L. BOYER

First printing 2026

E-Book ISBN 979-8-9884029-7-8
Paperback ISBN 979-8-9884029-8-5

PROLOGUE

"It's so good to get away from everything. The heat has been terrible at home, so I'm glad we decided to head to the mountains, even if it is the Great Smokies instead of the Rockies." She punched him in his right arm.

"I'm with you, babe. Work has been busy now that oil rigs are up and running again. I hope it will stay that way for a while."

"I hope it does, so we can start saving for a down payment on a house. With the interest rates high, it will take a large down payment so we can afford the mortgage."

They were on their way to an Airbnb Rachel had found online in the NC mountains. She's glad her mom agreed to take their dog, Rusty. He would have enjoyed the mountains, but they were nervous about him getting into a scrape with a snake or bear. She had been reading about the bear population in the Smokies. She learned that they are not aggressive, but you don't want to test one."

Evan was driving in a low gear, trying to get up the steepest mountain road they had managed so far. Suddenly, Evan braked when they saw a large rock, more like a boulder, in the middle of the road. It was positioned so there was no room to get around it. He decided to get out and see if there was any way at all.

"Rachel, would you get me a tire iron out of the back. Do you know where it is?"

"Sure." She slipped on her old Sketchers and got out of the car. She looked down the ravine and saw they were on very steep, precarious ground. She removed the tire iron and handed it to Evan.

He knew it was probably futile, but tried using the iron as a lever to budge the boulder; he was unsuccessful.

"I'm not going to be able to move it. I'm afraid that if we stay too long, another car might hit us, and then we will be in trouble. I want to get out of here."

"I agree. What do you want me to do?" asked Rachel.

"Just get back in the passenger seat, and we will try to back up to a place where we can turn around. These cars can turn on a dime." They were driving their four-year-old Subaru.

Rachel did as Evan told her. She was nervous about this road, especially the ravine. "Just be careful."

"I know." He put the car in reverse and backed toward the mountain first, but there was not enough space to make a complete turn in front of the ravine.

"I'm going to try to turn the other way. It is our best chance. There is more berm on the ravine side."

He gently reversed his position and turned the car to back toward the ravine. It took several maneuvers, but he felt they were in good shape. He reversed again and felt the guardrail. He tried moving forward, but the car's bumper was stuck. When he moved forward, the car slid sideways, and he lost control. Rachel screamed. That was the last sound he heard.

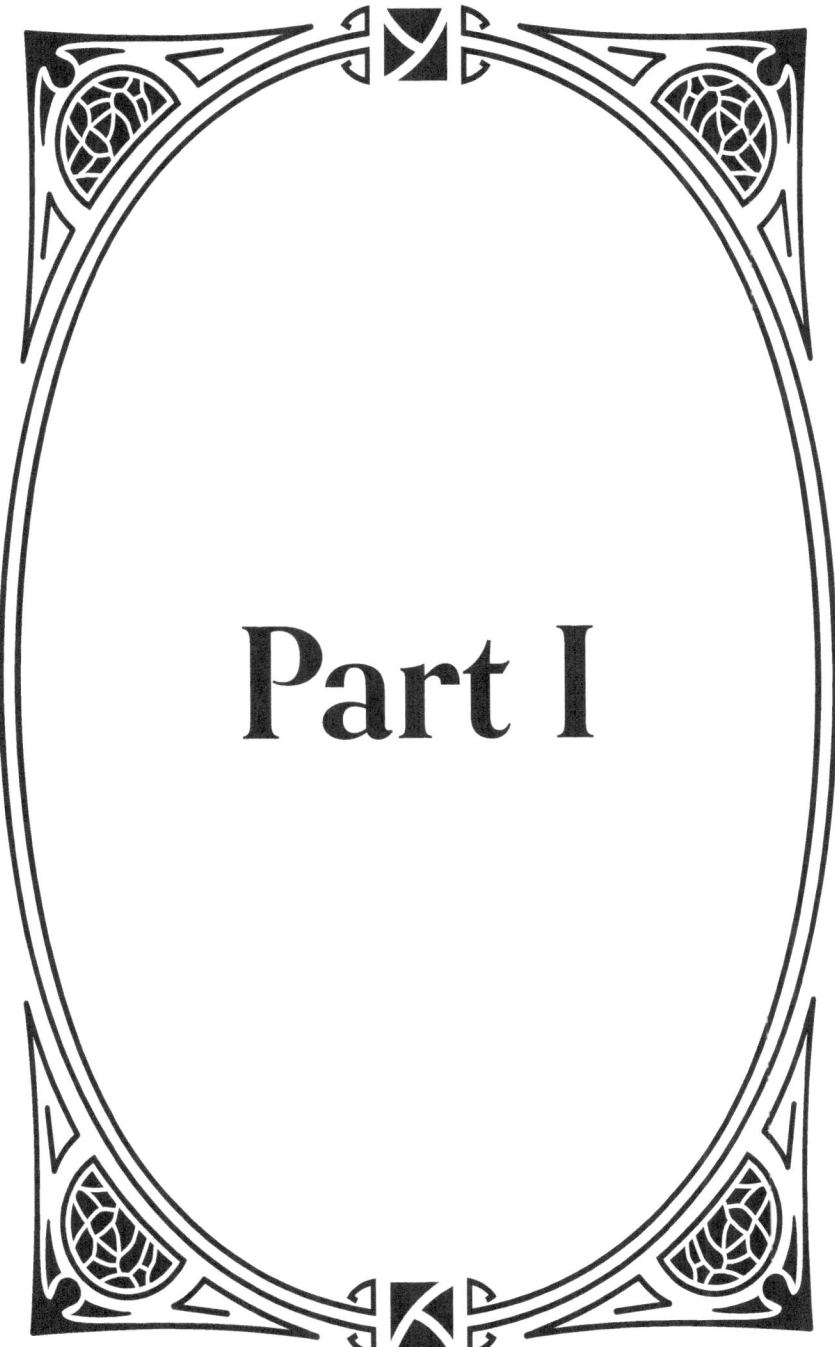

Part I

CHAPTER

1

Ally and Neal were getting ready for dinner on the last night of the cruise, which happened to be the night they were invited to sit at the Captain's Table. Ally had packed her long black dress, with a left-side slit that reached up to her thigh. She was glad she had remembered to pack her best silk stockings. The dress featured a low back and a high jeweled neckline. She was wearing the beautiful diamond earrings Neal had given her as a wedding gift.

When her mother saw them just before the wedding, all she could say was, "Wow," as she admired them. "He has good taste. You picked well, Ally," said her mother, Gloria.

"You have such a soft way of saying the obvious," said her sister, Janet. Ally laughed at both of them. They were there helping her put the final touches on her bridal trousseau before the wedding.

Ally couldn't believe she was about to take such a big step at her age. She never thought she would get married, and why should she? She and Neal had been dating for three years. They each had a home. They were financially independent and compatible, especially in areas that mattered. The only argument she remembered was when she got sick with COVID a couple of years ago. She thought he was making too much fuss over her then, but she had to admit that she liked the attention.

The real reason she was marrying him was the right one: she was in love. Head over heels, she knew he felt the same way about her. Neither of them wanted to be apart. It had been getting harder and harder to say goodbye at the end of a weekend whenever he had to drive back to Raleigh to get ready for his anesthesia rotation. He finally came to her a couple of months ago and told her that his accountant said he could retire very comfortably, and so he did. He put the house in Raleigh up for sale and made a nice net profit. His beach house was paid for, so he used some of his windfall to remodel it. Shortly after that, he walked her down to the beach in front of his house, got down on one knee, and proposed. She wasn't expecting it. After shedding tears and choking up, she finally said, "Yes!" He told her she made him the happiest man in the world. That was last October, and now it is May. The next day, they would board a plane in Rome and fly back home, where they would live as husband and wife.

The dinner was perfect that evening. It consisted of fresh red snapper, accompanied by fresh asparagus and golden potatoes, all cooked to perfection. The appetizers were bruschetta with fresh tomatoes and mozzarella, and the aperitif was Campari. The sommelier served them three wines, each to their taste. The dry was Ally and Neal's favorite.

After the meal, they complimented the staff and thanked the captain for a beautiful evening. Then, they proceeded to the dance floor on the top deck. They tended to prefer 40s music in the late evening. Sometimes, Ally insisted they go to a disco room. It was music she grew up on. In Manhattan, where she spent her career as a nurse, she enjoyed going to clubs and dancing all night. They spent the rest of the evening dancing under the stars as the ship made its way to their final destination. Neal was the first to say, "I think it is time to head to our room, darling." She never got tired of hearing him say those words.

Ally chuckled, "I agree."

They had a couple of friends they enjoyed hanging out with, so they exchanged emails before leaving, but it was unlikely they would see them again, since they were from New Zealand. Still, it wouldn't have been polite to leave without at least exchanging contact information.

They walked to the elevator that would carry them to the Lido deck, then to the port-side elevator that would take them to their stateroom. When they arrived at their room for the last time, Ally noticed their suite number was 3013. She suddenly felt a chill, even though she had seen those numbers every day since they arrived ten days ago. She felt like something strange awaited them when they returned to North Carolina.

They enjoyed sitting out on the balcony; the quietness and solitude were hypnotic. Ally never appreciated stargazing until she moved to North Carolina. She paid more attention to the sky and the ocean than she ever had in her life. "Could we spend more time on the balcony than usual? I want to remember this evening for a very long time."

"Anything you want," said Neal.

"I'm going to slip into something more comfortable," she winked at him.

She had packed for their return flight earlier in the day, so they wouldn't have much to do tonight. She changed into the lavender negligee that Eliza had given her at the bridal shower. Everyone she worked with had been fantastic. She was thankful she worked for such a great company. Three Island Catering, her employer, was a job she had never dreamed she would be doing at this time in her life.

She was let go from her RN position in New York after refusing to get the vaccine. She was exposed to COVID-19 patients for months, and she felt she had built up antibodies. She was never opposed to vaccines, like the flu shot, which she was required to receive every year. However, when the unvetted COVID vaccine became available and was being pushed on the hospital staff, she felt compelled to take a stand.

She was fortunate to have a place to go. Her grandmother, Harriet, had a beach house in NC, where Ally and her siblings spent many summers. When she passed, it was left to her only child, Ally's mother. When Ally became 'homeless', her mother offered the beach house to her, and her siblings had no issue with it. They lived in different states and didn't have the time or the desire to use it. Her parents now live in Bartow, Florida, after her father sold his pharmacy in Eldridge, New York, where she and her siblings had grown up. The beach was no longer a draw for them. Her father golfed up until recently. He was in the late stages of Alzheimer's now, so he was no longer able to play. Her mother played bridge and cards when she could, but caring for her father had become her priority. Ally had long been concerned for her father. As a nurse, she noticed the signs of Alzheimer's early and urged her mother to take him to his doctor, which she did.

The doctor prescribed medications to slow the progression of the disease, but they were told there was no cure. Her mother remembered when they were first married, how she helped take care of her father's mother, who had dementia. After Janet, her sister, was born, they had to move her into a nursing home. She lingered there for about a year, she had been told when she was older. She never knew her father's mother because, being the youngest child, she had passed before she was born.

She joined Neal on the balcony. He had changed into his pajama pants and the silk robe she had given him for his birthday. His initials had been monogrammed on it. He joked that he felt like Hugh Hefner. Everyone got a great laugh out of that.

Their families had come together nicely. Neal had one son from a previous marriage. Eric lived in Pinehurst, North Carolina, and was a dentist. He hadn't married yet, but had a girlfriend he had been seeing for a couple of years. Neal thought he might be proposing soon. Ally liked Charlotte the first time she met her. They bonded over being cat lovers. Ally's cat, Lucky, was being cared for by her best friend, Mary Hughes, whom she met upon moving to the beach house. They have had both happy and sad times together. Within a couple of weeks of moving to NC, Ally learned that a human skeleton had washed up on the beach she lived closest to. It turned out to be a nursing student who had gone missing while at college in Syracuse, New York. Her name was Katie Edwards, and Ally knew her even though she was in the class below hers. She often wondered what had happened to her. She learned from the news that Katie's parents lived nearby, and she reached them through the Brunswick Sheriff's Office. Once she made contact, they worked together to find out what had happened to her. At least what the police assumed happened. They believed she was the victim of a serial killer who had been caught but was killed in prison prior to Katie's remains being found.

Mary Hughes, her new friend, was her sounding board during this time and was there when they realized there was no finality in Katie's case. Still, they learned about her life outside of school, and her parents were so pleased that their daughter had done a kindness for a family that needed it so badly. She was remembered fondly, and that mattered more to them.

Mary, as it turned out, had a mystery of her own, so Ally helped her to find out what had happened to her husband's aunt, Mary Littlejohn. It was a very unusual case, but through perseverance and a bit of luck, aided by DNA, they discovered that his Aunt Mary had a living son.

Before Ally started planning her wedding, she and Mary flew to Atlanta, met with detectives at the Atlanta PD, and explained everything they had discovered. Essentially, it had been determined that Mary Littlejohn had staged her own disappearance. She left a letter to her son, Michael, which he found in her safety deposit box after her death. The cold-case detectives expressed their appreciation for the information. The case had been cold for more than fifty years. Now, with the information they had been given, they could bring it to a close by conducting their own investigation to confirm what Ally and Mary had told them. Her husband's aunt was dead, but not before she had a whole life and raised a wonderful son.

Sitting on the balcony chair, she said to Neal, "I had not noticed our room number until we came back tonight."

"Oh yeah, what about it?" Neal asked.

"It is 3013. It has the number thirteen. It gives me the creeps."

"I thought they avoided the number 13 in most buildings, such as hotels, like skipping a floor. I guess that doesn't apply to room numbers."

"I thought they did too. I wonder where that got started? The number 13 must be very creepy for a lot of reasons."

"Well, let me see if I can make it a little creepier." He stood, took her hand, and invited her to stand. He immediately pulled her close and kissed her deeply. Why don't we take this little creepy party to bed?"

"Aye, Aye, Captain." Ally saluted Neal.

They crawled into the bed, which the staff had turned back earlier. There were mints on the pillows. The sheets were so soft. Ally had noted it the first night and wanted to purchase the same kind when she got home. She had been meaning to change linens for a while, anyway.

Neal kissed her neck and ears as he felt up her leg. He slipped her gown off her shoulders and exposed her breasts. He was hard and more than ready. His thrusts started slowly because he wanted to enjoy her for as long as possible. The moonlight streamed in through the open balcony, and he could see her face. She was beautiful, and he was so happy that he would wake up every morning for the rest of his life and see that face. Her moans increased, causing him to increase his thrusts. As he spilled his fluids into her, she cried out as she reached an orgasm. He smiled and collapsed on top of her. He whispered in her ear, "Are you satisfied?"

"Yes, darling. Always."

CHAPTER 2

They arrived at the Atlanta airport and planned to spend the night with Ally's college roommate and friend, Diedre.

"I am so happy to be back on US soil," said Ally.

"I am, too," said Neal. "You need to call Diedre, don't you? We could get an Uber to her house. I'll pull up my app."

Ally looked at her phone and saw she had forty-two voicemails, mostly from her mother and sister.

"Oh no. I hope nothing happened to my father."

"Why, what's wrong?" asked Neal.

After disembarking, they were almost at customs, but Ally wanted to listen to a message, so she stepped out of line.

The voicemail was from Janet, her sister. She said, "Ally, I need you. Something has happened. Please call as soon as you get this message." Ally heard the crack in her sister's voice and knew it was not good news. Her knees went weak.

She listened to a couple of other messages, and the request was the same in each. Her mother left a message saying, "Your sister and I need you to call as soon as you get this message."

Neal closed the Uber app and looked at his text messages; the last one was from Adam, Ally's brother-in-law. It read: *Call immediately, URGENT.*

"I got a text message from Adam asking me to call immediately."

Ally looked at him, and all of the color had drained from her face. Neal found a security guard and asked for a chair or a place for his wife to sit. They complied immediately.

Ally was crying, "I cannot believe I was gone on my honeymoon when my father died. I know that has to be it."

Neal told her he would call Adam right now to find out. "Please try to calm down until we know what this is about, okay?"

Ally nodded her head.

Neal stepped away and dialed Adam's number. He picked up on the first ring. "Hello, Neal?"

"Yes, we just got into Hartsfield and have all of these messages. What has happened?"

Adam said, "Rachel is missing."

"Rachel?" asked Neal.

"Yes, she and her boyfriend, Evan, left three days ago to go to an Airbnb in North Carolina, but never made it. Their phones pinged in a remote area where Hurricane Helene had caused damage, and search parties had found nothing. We are getting ready to go to the airport."

"Where will you be flying into?" asked Neal.

"Charlotte. We'll arrive at seven pm. Janet is beside herself, as you can imagine, and so is everyone else. I'd like Ally to meet us there, if that is possible. Gloria can't leave John right now."

"So, he is okay?"

"Yes, yes. They are fine. Gloria hasn't told him about Rachel."

"I tell you what, let me talk with Ally and we will see about getting a flight from here to Charlotte, hopefully one that will arrive about the same time you do. I'll call you right back."

"Thanks," said Adam.

Neal weighed how he would break this news to Ally. He knew her niece meant the world to her. Rachel had followed in Ally's footsteps, becoming a nurse. Since then, they have become very close.

"Ally, it's not about your father." He was bending down in front of her. She had her head hanging down and was crying."

"Are you sure? Well, what is it?"

"It's Rachel. She's missing with her boyfriend. They left three days ago for a vacation in North Carolina and never made it to the Airbnb. There has been a search started in the area where her phone pinged last, but it's close to an area affected by Hurricane Helene."

"Oh, my God. Not Rachel, please not Rachel."

"Your sister and Adam are boarding a plane soon to fly into Charlotte and would like you to meet them there. Is that something you would be up to?"

"Yes, yes, of course."

"Good, let's get through this line and get to a kiosk so I can get us tickets to Charlotte."

"Okay."

Ally stood up, shaking all over, but she grabbed Neal's hand and said, "Let's go."

****

Neal retrieved their luggage, and they went to the Delta check-in counter to pick up their boarding passes and recheck them. Ally was by his side, but she was unable to think and slow to react. Neal could see the expression on the employee's face, and he mouthed, "She's okay." The check-in clerk nodded and smiled.

Their flight was at four eighteen, so they didn't have much time. They rushed to the gate, and boarding had already started. He texted Adam to let him know they had a flight and shared their arrival time, then put his phone on airplane mode. He will remind Ally to do the same when they are settled on the plane.

Once they were settled and airborne, Ally let out a sigh.

"I know she is going to be found. It's probably just a misunderstanding. Maybe they decided to stay somewhere else," she said.

Neal wondered if she had forgotten about the phone pinging. He didn't want to bring it up. Let sleeping dogs lie, but secretly, he hoped she was right.

It was a quick flight with barely enough time for the flight attendants to give out refreshments. He asked Ally if she wanted wine, but she declined.

The captain announced they were about ten minutes out and instructed the flight attendants to prepare the cabin for landing. They had been dozing, and it startled them both. Then Ally remembered why they were on this plane and started crying again.

Neal had called Diedra while they were waiting for the luggage and told her what was going on. She wanted to speak with Ally, but he told her she was too upset right now. She accepted that and told him to keep her updated. She told him she would start a prayer chain at their church.

After hanging up with Diedra, he called Mary Hughes, Ally's neighbor and friend. He reached her voicemail and left a message stating that they were delayed and would not be coming in the next day. He assured her that he would let her know as soon as possible when they would catch a flight. He knew she would wonder why Ally didn't call, but he figured she would call Ally later anyway.

CHAPTER 3

After disembarking and collecting their luggage, Ally ordered an Uber, which took them to the downtown Marriott, where they would stay and wait for Janet and Adam. After checking in, Neal had Ally lie down, and he retrieved two mini bottles of Glenlivet from the minibar. He poured each of them a drink without ice and insisted Ally drink some, which she finally did. She was asleep ten minutes later.

He texted Adam their room number. He added, If you have trouble getting on the elevator, call me.

An hour later, he heard a tap on the door. He nudged Ally on her shoulder and answered the door. A sorrowful and pale Janet and Adam were standing there.

"Come in, please," said Neal as he stepped back.

Ally stood up and ran to Janet, and they cried, not wanting to let go of one another. Adam set their carry-on down, and then they collapsed in a heap on the floor. Neal was at his side, encouraging him to sit in the chair. He got both of them a bottle of water out of their mini-fridge.

"I have something stronger if you need it, Adam."

"Not now, maybe later."

Ally sat Janet down on the other bed and asked, "What do they know?"

"Not much. They were driving Evan's Subaru, a reliable car with new tires and a recent check-up. I verified it with Rachel. I don't think they had car trouble."

"They could have had a flat tire," said Adam.

"Of course, but I'm trying to focus on the positive things," said Janet in a terse tone of voice. Ally thought, *I have never heard them speak to each other that way.*

Neal said, "When did you last get an update?" trying to change the subject.

"Just before we boarded the plane, I received a call, and there wasn't any positive news. They really don't have a focus on where to search. The cell phone ping wasn't specific enough, and the area is a dense forest. I know they are doing all they can, but we are at a loss. We don't know anything about the North Carolina mountains," he scoffed.

"You're doing all you can do, Adam. The authorities will find them. How well did y'all know her boyfriend?"

"We were around him several times. They were, after all, living together. He seemed responsible and was crazy about Rachel."

There wasn't much else to say. The realization of what was happening was weighing on all of them.

Ally asked Janet, "Do they know you are here, that you flew up?"

"Yes, we are to meet with the sheriff's office tomorrow morning. You'll go with us, yes?"

"Of course," Ally said. She remembered she needed to call her friend, Mary.

"Neal, I'm going to call Mary," said Ally.

"I left her a voicemail. You could wait until tomorrow if you're too tired."

"Okay, I'll deal with it tomorrow."

****

They didn't get much sleep. They decided to share a room because no one wanted to be alone. Ally was worried about her sister; after all, Rachel was her only daughter. The next morning, it was a bit hectic dressing in shifts, but they managed. Ally and Janet didn't put on makeup, which helped save time. After a quick cup of coffee at the lobby restaurant, Neal approached the concierge and explained that they needed a rental car.

"No worries, sir. I will get you a car in a few minutes. There is a rental agency across the street."

Neal thanked him and provided the necessary information, along with his American Express card. Once everything was verified and the documents were signed, they were instructed to wait in the lobby; the doorman would notify them when the car arrived.

****

They had to get a large car because of the luggage, mainly Neal and Ally's. The Lexus was roomy and comfortable. Neal searched for the Sheriff of Bluffton's station on his phone, found an address, and entered it into the car's GPS. It was only about ninety minutes northwest of them. A little over one hundred miles. His calculated mind told him that this was going to be a rough ride, in more ways than one.

When they arrived at the station, a local news truck from Charlotte was already there. The news of a missing couple from Texas had caused quite a stir. Ally grabbed Neal's hand when she saw them. She was comfortable with the news media, having experienced it firsthand in the Katie Morgan case. She experienced it with Katie's parents; it wasn't too bad, but in this instance, it was personal, and she felt more pressure.

They entered the Sheriff's department through the front door and were greeted by the receptionist. She told them the Sheriff would be right with them. A few minutes passed, and a tall man with a mustache and light brown hair entered the lobby. He introduced himself as Sheriff Mark Bowen. He asked them to follow him into the conference room. An FBI agent introduced himself as Agent Jay

Camp. Another deputy was in the room, and he introduced himself to them as Deputy Tim Cox.

"I don't have any news for you all at this time," stated Sheriff Bowen. We have had the birds, that is, the helicopters, flying up and down the stretch of main road near where the cell phone pinged. There was a large rock, more of a boulder, on the road we believe they would have been traveling. There is speculation that they may have turned around upon seeing it. If they did, they may have over-estimated their space, leaving little room to get around it. We were notified of it in the morning, we believe, when they were traveling, but had not had time to remove it or put up detour warnings. These things happen, and most of the time, there are no issues. The roads are dangerous, and when you climb an incline, you need to drop into a lower gear to slow down. I've never had an instance where some-one actually hit one. Of course, coming from the other direction is another story. Going down the mountain is treacherous, but if you aren't speeding, there is enough time to stop. Additionally, there are signs throughout the area warning of falling rocks."

"There is no sign of them?" asked Janet. Her voice was pleading with the Sheriff.

"I wish I had more, Mrs. Butler. We are still searching, but it is treacherous. Several volunteers regularly conduct searches and come out to help. I have also taken a few calls from their friends in Texas, who wanted to travel here and help with the search. I don't discourage it, but I remind them that we have search teams quite accustomed to the terrain, and it might be dangerous for someone not physically used to this hilly country, but I cannot tell them not to come."

"We understand, Sheriff," said Adam.

"I need to ask you," said Agent Camp, "do you have any reason to think Evan or Rachel would have anyone who may want to harm them?"

"No, I don't think so," said Janet. "Should we be thinking about that? I mean, does that happen?"

"Well, not so much. However, you never know with younger people who are not experienced travelers. Could they have gotten mixed up in a gang or a drug situation? It isn't very likely, but it's not out of the question. That's why I'm here."

"You're here because of drugs or gangs?" asked Neal.

"Not just that, but since they drove from Texas, they went through many states to get here. There are human trafficking smugglers all along those routes."

Janet screamed so loud that it startled all of them. "No, no, no, not my baby. I cannot bear to think of her being kidnapped and sold for sex trafficking."

Ally immediately went to her sister's side and tried calming her down.

"Mrs. Butler," Agent Camp said. "I truly didn't mean to make it sound like that was a probability, because it isn't."

"Then why did you mention it?" Adam screamed at Agent Camp.

"I only mentioned it because there are multiple states involved, and the FBI gets involved anytime there is a possibility of a kidnapping. That is all, and I apologize for bringing it up now. I know you're just being brought into this investigation, while the rest of us have been working on it for three days, ever since you called the Airbnb and discovered they hadn't arrived. Please forgive my callous remarks."

Everyone seemed to cool down. Neal even noticed the room felt much cooler. Sheriff Bowen asked Deputy Cox if he had anything to add. "Not at this time, Sheriff."

Sheriff Bowen asked where they were staying, and Neal handed him his card and the address.

"Dr?" Mark asked.

"Retired anesthesiologist."

"We could use you around here. Doctors, dentists, and surgeons are all in short supply. It took me six months to get in for an eye exam."

Neal laughed and said, "Unless you need to be put under for some reason, I am of no use."

Ally laughed and said, "But you are great at other things." She looked at the Sheriff and said, "We are newlyweds."

"Well, congratulations," they all chimed in.

Ally blushed and said, "Thanks."

Adam rose and tapped Janet on her forearm, indicating she should get up with him. Neal and Ally also stood. "We should go," Adam said.

"We will update you on anything, and again, I think I can speak for the rest of us; we are so sorry that you are having to go through this."

Adam hung his head in defeat and said, "We are too."

They all walked out, Adam leading the way and Neal bringing up the rear.

Once they got to the car, Ally said, "I'd like to sit with Janet on the way back."

Janet nodded, and they got in the back seat.

"Where to?" asked Neal.

"Lunch," said Ally.

They stopped at a roadside BBQ restaurant. None of them was hungry, but they needed something to eat and to talk about the next steps.

"I feel that we should stay a few more days, in case something is found. I want to be nearby in case anything happens. I know that doesn't sound good, and I hope and pray they are found alive. I want to be close by in case they need anything. What about DNA? Do they need DNA from us? No one said anything," said Janet.

Ally said they might need it later. "Have you all sent in your DNA to one of those sites the police use?"

"No, but we will. I'll go online tonight and find one. It might be important one day."

Neal looked at Adam, and he could see he was about to break down. "What are you thinking, Adam?"

"I am thinking that I don't want to face losing my little girl, and I'm afraid that's what is going to happen. What if she is lying out there somewhere, and animals get her?"

No one said anything.

Ally asked, "Have you been in touch with Evan's parents?"

"It's only his mother; his dad died in Afghanistan. She is distraught. He has a brother named Eric; in fact, they are identical twins. She'll never be the same. She doesn't have the means to travel at the moment. Also, she is helping to take care of her mother, who has Alzheimer's, and she works two jobs herself. I will see her when we return. She doesn't live far from us."

They drove back to Charlotte, each lost in their thoughts. Ally wondered whether Janet had called their mother, but didn't want to bring it up.

Ally and Neal decided to stay one more night, so they checked back into the Marriott. This time, Adam and Janet got a separate room. The next morning, Adam and Neal went over to the rental agency to transfer the car into Adam's name. Neal booked a flight for him and Ally to Myrtle Beach, where Mary will meet them.

At the airport, Ally gave Janet a huge hug and told her how much she loved her and Rachel. "I'm sure Justin is a wreck, also," said Ally.

"He is, and so is his wife. I don't know how I'm going to go on without my Rachel."

"I know. Did you order the DNA kits?"

"I did. They'll be there when we get home. I want to stay a few more days. Maybe something good will happen," she said with tears in her eyes.

Neal said, "We need to go in order to make our flight."

They walked into the airport terminal. Ally hoped by the time she got home, Rachel would have called her mother and said, "*I am sorry, Mom. We just had to stop and see this cool place. I wish you were here.*"

CHAPTER 4

When they got to their gate and found a seat, Ally told Neal she needed to call Mary. She walked over to a corner so she could have a quiet conversation with her friend.

"Hi, Mary. I'm sorry I haven't called you. I have been upset by the news we received when we arrived in Atlanta. It is awful."

"What is it, Ally. Are you two okay? Did something happen on the cruise?" asked Mary.

"No, nothing like that. When we arrived yesterday from Rome, I had several messages waiting for me from my mother and sister."

"Oh, no. Your father?"

"No, much worse. It's about my sister's daughter. You remember, Rachel, she went to Baylor University and became a nurse? She followed in my footsteps."

"Yes."

"She's missing."

"What? How?"

"She and her boyfriend were going on a car trip to the North Carolina mountains and were going to stay in an Airbnb, disconnect for a few days. You know what I mean. Just a vacay."

"Okay, and?"

"They never checked in. Her phone pinged in an area that Hurricane Helene had damaged. There's a lot of debris left behind, so they are searching in the area where the phone pinged. However, the forest is dense, and they're having trouble finding any wreckage. There are several volunteers on the ground, and I'm sure they are doing all they can do."

Ally was crying and searching through her pockets for a tissue.

"I am so sorry, dear. How is your sister holding up?"

"Not well. We all met with the sheriff, a deputy, and an FBI agent yesterday, and they outlined all the measures being taken. Helicopters, K9s, searchers. Everything possible. It is going to take time. Janet and Adam are going to stay a few days, but Neal and I are at the airport, and the plane leaves at three-forty. Do you want us to take an Uber?"

"No, I will be there to pick you up. What is the flight number and Airline?"

"Delta, 2019. Thank you so much, Mary. It will be so good to see you."

"Okay, I'll see you later and will pray for all of you. I love you. Tell Neal I love him, too."

"I will and thank you."

Ally sat next to Neal and told him that Mary would pick them up. He reached over and took her hand. "I know how upset you are. We'll get through this together."

She lay her head on his shoulder and fell into a light sleep. The sun was setting, and the airport took on an amber glow. She tried keeping her heavy lids open, but couldn't manage it. She dreamed of hearing the news from her sister that she had a niece. It was a great day. She knew her mother would be thrilled. She already had a grandson and now a baby girl. Life was good.

The next thing she knew, Neal was tapping her shoulder, saying, "Wake up, sleepyhead. It's time to board."

She stretched, then stood up fast and lost her balance. She had to sit back down before she fell into the lap of the man sitting next to her. Neal was bent over picking up his carry-on when it happened.

Ally was embarrassed and apologized to the man. "No worries, Miss. I hope you're okay."

"I will be," Ally smiled at him.

While on the plane, she and Neal spoke only of the tragedy that awaited them. "I have to be there for Janet. We were never very close, probably because of the age difference, but as we got older, those years didn't matter anymore, and we grew closer. Sisters should support one another in times of need."

"I completely agree. You do whatever you think is best. If you want to go to Texas, that is fine. I'm sure Gene will work with you."

"Gene is the best. I don't know how I would have made it without him. He took a chance when he hired me, but I think he is happy he did. I have the best friends in North Carolina, and as a bonus, I found the love of my life."

"Oh, really, who is that?" he teased her.

She gave him 'that' look. "You know it's you, silly."

He grinned and gave her a peck on the forehead.

The flight attendant passed by about then and smiled at Ally. "Lucky girl," she said.

"Lucky, I almost forgot about him. I can't wait to see him."

Lucky was the cat Ally adopted as a kitten when she first moved to her beach house. He showed up on the second day she was there, demanding to be let in. She had never had a pet before, but she fell in love with him and treated him like her baby.

"Yes, that darn cat. Who do you love more, me or Lucky?"

"That's a hard one," she laughed.

****

They retrieved their luggage, and Ally texted Mary to let her know they were ready to be picked up. She was at the curb as soon as they walked over to the door. She got out of the car and gave them both a hug. Neal let Ally sit in the front, and he stretched out in the back of Mary's comfortable Lexus.

"Are y'all hungry?"

"We should be, but not really. How about you, darling?" asked Ally.

"I could eat something, but don't stop on my account. How about a burger to take home?"

"We'll stop closer to home. How's that?" asked Mary.

"Sounds good."

"How's my other boyfriend?" asked Ally.

"Do you mean Winston?" Mary laughed.

"No, Lucky."

"I know, he is great. I went ahead and took him over to Neal's. He is in the mud room."

"Good," said Neal.

"Thank you for taking care of him, Mary, and everything else you do for me."

Mary looked over at her and said, "You know, I'd do anything for you."

The traffic was heavy in Myrtle Beach, but as soon as Mary could, she got on the bypass to get around all of the tourist traffic. They reached the North Carolina state line about thirty minutes later.

Ally asked, "Mary, did you ever do your DNA?"

"You know I did. Remember, after we found Michael. My son ordered a kit for me. You were too busy getting ready for the wedding, so I may have forgotten to mention it. I got the results back in just about six weeks. Nothing unusual. No horse thieves that I know of, anyway. All of my sons have done theirs, and most of my daughters-in-law."

"Did you upload to one of the Gen-match sites law enforcement uses?"

"I don't know. We all did Ancestry. Why do you ask?"

"I'm going to investigate and send mine into one of those that allow law enforcement to use. I think it would be a good thing to do."

"I agree, it would," said Mary. "Let me know, and perhaps I can send mine there, also."

"Okay, I will."

****

Mary dropped them off at Neal's and told Ally she would call her the next day.

Ally ran up the steps and went through the mudroom door to see Lucky. She picked him up and gave him several hugs. He let her do that for a few seconds, but then squirmed to get down. She opened the kitchen door and saw Neal coming out of the elevator with the luggage. He had an elevator installed before the wedding, mainly for Ally's parents. Her father was fragile and showing more and more signs of Alzheimer's disease. He knew it broke Ally's heart.

The family was amazed at how he managed to walk his youngest daughter down the beach path to give her away. In that moment, he felt John knew exactly what he was doing, but he wasn't sure he would remember a few moments later. That was the way the disease worked; it robbed so much from the person unfortunate enough to be struck down by it.

After the suitcases were open and on the guest bed, Ally started looking for her cosmetic bag. She only wanted a shower and then to get ready for bed. Tonight was going to be their first night as husband and wife. She just wished it were in a better spirit. There was a pall hanging over them.

They had been asleep for just about an hour when Ally's phone rang. When she saw it was from Janet, she put her hand on Neal and said, "Wake up. It's Janet."

"Hello, Janet?"

"Yes, it's me. We just heard they believe they have found their car. They won't be able to reach it until daylight, but one of the searches confirmed it is a Subaru. I'm so scared, Ally. The sheriff is sending his technician to our hotel first thing in the morning to collect a DNA swab. I just got off the phone with Marilyn, Evan's mom, and she got a call from the local police about coming out and getting a swab from her, as well."

"It's protocol, Janet. I know you're upset. I wish I could comfort you. Have you been in touch with your church?"

"Yes, our minister is aware, and the church prayer chain is active. I know everyone wants the best outcome, but I don't believe we are going to get what we want: our child and her boyfriend alive and well."

"I know. I've put you on speaker so that Neal can hear."

"Janet, is Adam nearby?"

"I'm here, Neal. It isn't good. The car was located in a ravine, approximately 400 feet below where they were driving. There are guardrails along most of it, but hurricane-related damage has left some areas without them, or they are too fragile to be effective. I've been online reading stories about how treacherous the roads are in that area. I'm not sure why Evan and Rachel ignored the warnings. It's my fault. I should have looked into it for them. They are just a couple of young kids who only wanted to get away and be together."

Adam started wailing. "Neal, I need to hang up now," said Janet.

"I understand. We'll talk in the morning."

CHAPTER
5

Janet and Adam were awake all night. Unable to sleep, they held each other and cried, sure that they were going to get terrible news. Throughout their lives, they tried to be the best parents they could be. They never had any problems with either of their kids. The worst thing Janet ever had to do was ground Rachel for not cleaning her room. It took that one time, and she never had to do it again.

They were a church going family. The children attended Sunday School, Youth group, and various activities. Justin had gone to Haiti on a mission trip one summer when he was fourteen years old. They often wondered how lucky they were to have such great kids. Some of their friends' kids got into drugs, mostly marijuana. Many of them began drinking at a young age. To their knowledge, neither Justin nor Rachel ever did drugs. If they did, it was well hidden from them.

At six o'clock AM, the alarm went off, and Janet got up to make coffee. She showered and dressed. Adam followed her. They were dressed and ready when a call from the desk informed them that the Sheriff's Department had sent a technician to see them. Adam told them to allow them access to their floor.

A few minutes later, there was a tap on the door. Janet opened the door and found Justin, their son, standing there with a carry-on, accompanied by the technician.

Janet started crying and rushed into Justin's arms. He held his mother tight. "How did you know to come?" she asked him.

"I just did. I didn't want you and Dad to be alone, so I took the red eye last night and stayed at the airport until I thought it would be a good time to get a cab to your hotel. Dad sent me the address and room number to let me know where you were."

The technician introduced herself as Heather Monroe. She expressed her sympathies and explained that she needed to obtain the DNA sample for the lab.

After she was done collecting the samples, she told them she would drop them off at the lab in Charlotte. "I wish you well," she said as she exited the room.

"What do we do now?" asked Justin.

"We wait," his dad told him.

****

They went downstairs and asked the concierge for the best breakfast spot near the hotel.

"Right around the corner. When you exit, go right and take the first right. You will see Ella's. Delicious blueberry pancakes."

"Thank you," said Adam.

They did as the concierge instructed and found Ella easily. There was a short wait, but after they had coffee and ordered, they could relax.

Janet kept looking at her phone. "Mom, I want you to know Ellen, and I went to mass the night before last and lit a candle for Rachel and Evan."

"Thank you."

Ellen was Catholic, and when she married Justin, he converted to make her happy. Her family was of Mexican heritage and took their religion very seriously. Family was everything to them. Janet had grown to accept that her grandchildren would be Catholics, and she was okay with it. Adam didn't have an opinion. He only wanted Justin to be happy and hoped he would one day be a father.

On their walk back to the hotel, Adam noticed a Bluffton sheriff's vehicle parked in front of them. He became emotional and took Janet's hand. He wasn't sure if she had seen it.

"Do you think they are waiting for us?"

"I do," Adam said.

When they arrived in the hotel lobby, Adam saw the Sheriff sitting in a chair. He looked up at them, and Adam noted the somber expression on his face.

Janet started trembling. She leaned into Justin, and he and Adam held her up. When they got closer to the Sheriff, he stood up.

Sheriff Bowen said to them, "I am so sorry to tell you this, but the remains of a young female and male were discovered this morning. They were inside the Subaru, which we have identified as the male's. The registration was in the glove compartment, and his ID was in his pocket. We still have to complete the autopsies and confirm the identities through DNA, but we're fairly certain we located your loved ones."

Janet wailed, collapsing on the floor. Immediately, a wheelchair appeared, and a woman who identified herself as a nurse helped her into it. Adam thanked her and said they would go up to their room. The sheriff followed them to the elevator. Adam tried holding his emotions in check because he knew his wife and son would need him.

Once they were in the room, Adam picked Janet up with Justin's help and laid her on the bed. He then put the wheelchair in the hallway. He motioned to the sheriff to step out in the hallway, out of earshot of Janet. Justin joined them. Adam suspected his son was being stoic. Justin was always able to hold his emotions intact.

"Where do we go from here, Sheriff Bowen?" asked Adam.

"It will be a couple of days before the autopsies are completed, but the DNA match should be back by this evening. It will be preliminary, but it will be enough to confirm."

"Do you need us to stay? I mean, do I need to go to the morgue?"

"I was going to ask if you could do that as well."

"Of course, whatever you need."

"I can take you and bring you back if that would be okay?" said Sheriff Bowen.

"I can stay with Mom," said Justin.

"Okay, that's good. Yes, let me go in and tell her where I am going," said Adam.

****

They drove in silence for a while. Adam broke the silence and asked the sheriff if he had lost a child.

"No, I haven't. I have had to break sad news to so many people, and every time I do, it takes a piece of my heart."

"Thank you for saying that. I don't think I have any of my heart left. It has splintered inside of me." Adam started crying.

They arrived at the morgue, located in a large hospital near Bluffton. The sheriff signed them in, and he and Adam headed for the elevator, which would take them downstairs to the morgue.

The technician scanned their identification passes and went to the storage units where Adam's daughter and her boyfriend now lie. They opened the first one, and it was Evan's body. Completely nude, with a sheet covering him. The technician pulled the sheet from Evan's face, and Adam put his hands to his face and nodded.

The technician repeated the procedure for the second unit, and before they pulled the sheet back, Adam dropped to his knees and said a prayer. He stood up and nodded for the technician to proceed. As soon as he saw her hair, he knew it was his beautiful Rachel. She had beautiful, sun-streaked, light-brown hair. He saw the scratches on her forehead and what looked to be shards of glass. Her face was swollen, and her bottom lip had blood caked on it. He knew she would bite her lips when she was stressed. He couldn't take any more. He nodded to the sheriff and turned away. He walked to the exit door as fast as he could.

CHAPTER

6

Ally received the phone call she dreaded; it was Adam. Janet was too distraught to talk with her. He told her that he made the identification at the morgue. The DNA was still being processed for both of them, but there was no doubt that it was them.

"She looked like an angel, only with some scratches and swelling of the face."

"That must have been difficult," said Ally.

"Yes, it was, but it needed to be done. By the way, Justin surprised us and flew in overnight. He arrived at the hotel first thing this morning."

"That's great. He is so thoughtful, and I know he must be so upset."

"He stayed with Janet while I went to the morgue with Sheriff Bowen."

"Has mom been updated?"

"I called her and my mom a few minutes ago. They will call other family members."

"Good, I'll call her later. When do you want me and Neal to come?"

"As soon as you can, Ally. Janet will need you, and Gloria needs to take care of your dad. He's not doing well. Since your wedding, he has taken at least one fall. Nothing broken, luckily."

"Oh my, he has gone down. He was very fragile at the wedding. We'll make arrangements to be there soon. I'll call her and see if she needs us to go there first. I'm sure Craig would want to be with you and Janet if he can arrange his schedule. He should definitely be at the services."

"That would be helpful," said Adam. "I'd better go. I'll call you later."

Neal came in with a bag of bagels. "Did I hear you on the phone?"

"Yes, it was Rachel and Evan. Adam did an identification of both bodies at the morgue this morning. Justin also flew in last night, so they are all together. We'll need to make arrangements to go to Texas or perhaps to Florida first to help my mother. Although I think Craig could and should fly to Texas with her. She will probably arrange for someone to stay with Dad."

"I'm so sorry." He came over and hugged her.

"I know. I had braced myself already. I need to call my mom. Adam told me my dad had fallen recently. She will need to make arrangements for him. I don't think he is in any condition to travel."

"I understand. Do what you need to do. You know I will be there for you."

****

"Hello, Mom? It's Ally."

"Hi, baby. How are you?"

"Sad, like you. Are you okay?"

"Not really, I'm still in bed. I let your dad sleep in this morning. He had a bad night. I haven't told him about Rachel, but it's like he knows something is wrong. He senses things."

"I don't doubt it. He is a sensitive guy, especially when it comes to his family."

"You're probably right. I'm walking into the study. I hope he doesn't wake up for a while," her mom said.

"I thought Neal and I would come down to your place, and then we could fly to Texas from there. Perhaps Craig could make the flight with us?"

"I'm not too sure about taking your father."

"I know, he's not well enough to travel. Adam told me about his fall."

"You're right. He's not in any shape to travel, Ally, especially to his granddaughter's funeral. I cannot handle both."

"Can you get help?"

"Yes, I've talked with his doctor, and he has sources and places where I can let him stay for a few days. I've already visited them and know other people who have used them. It won't be a problem."

Ally knew her mother to be very strong. She was an only child and came from a very wealthy family. She had high expectations of herself and her children. Ally didn't doubt that she had already checked everything out, so she would be prepared.

"I'll make arrangements for everything today and let you know our plans. Craig will go with me."

Her brother, Craig, was a Physical Therapist, specializing in Sports Medicine. He was working on his PhD.

After hanging up with her mom, Ally told Neal what they planned and that her dad wouldn't be going.

"I'll make our arrangements. You have enough on your mind. Don't forget to call Gene," he told her.

"Yeah, I should do that now. And Mary, too. I'll need her to take care of Lucky again."

****

Ally made her calls. Gene, her boss, told her to take as much time as she needed. He said they will get some temporary help. He told her how sorry he was and that he would tell Sarah what was going on. Sarah, his receptionist, had become the office manager. His business had grown exponentially since he put her in charge. He had no idea she had those skills. When Ally first applied there, she wasn't sure if she and Sarah would make a good fit. Ally thought she was a bit 'rough around the edges.' But she proved Ally wrong. She was a kind and caring person who had a rough upbringing, and she didn't come across as soft because she wasn't. Gene shared with Ally that Sarah grew up with drug addicted parents. She raised herself and her younger brother. They still lived together. "She has a trust issue," Gene said. "She doesn't have a boyfriend and isn't interested. I've tried fixing her up, but she refuses."

Ally could relate. She had been that way all of her life, for some reason. She dated many men in NYC; however, as soon as they started getting close, she found a reason to end the relationship. When she moved to North Carolina and met Neal, everything changed.

She called Mary, and she had many questions about the accident. Ally told her everything she knew. They have been through a lot together in the last three years and were as close as could be.

"Rachel and Evan were on a road they probably shouldn't have been on. They are novices at traveling alone, and even though it was treacherous, they probably thought of it as an adventure. The police have determined, from tire tracks, that they attempted to turn around. When they did, the tires caught the guardrail, and it didn't hold because of the slippery ground, allowing the car to lose traction. The momentum took over, and they crashed at the bottom of the ravine. There were so many limbs and debris from Helene that the car was camouflaged until the helicopter spotted something shiny. The sun must have been just right, casting its light. The search party was directed to that area, and even on the ground, it took them a little while to spot the car. By then, it was dark, and they could see that it was a Subaru, but they had to wait until daylight to finish the search. It was devastating."

"That's such a sad story. Just two young kids with their entire lives ahead of them. It makes me cry when I think about it. When is their funeral?" asked Mary.

"The date or dates have not been set. Now that I think about it, I wonder if they will hold their funerals together. It seems appropriate, don't you think?"

"I do, but it is the family's decision. They will make the right one. I'm so sorry. Don't worry about Lucky, he's my buddy."

After hanging up with Mary, Ally checked with Neal about travel arrangements.

"We are scheduled to fly out tomorrow around eleven, but have a layover in Atlanta."

"Would I have time to see Diedra?" asked Ally.

"No, it is only a half hour or so. I'm hoping our luggage gets transferred. We should arrive in Houston at six, but it will be five their time. Perhaps we could get Justin to pick us up? If not, it will be an Uber."

"Let's plan on an Uber. He may have a lot on him. Mother will also be flying in. Not sure when, but probably tomorrow sometime."

"That's fine." He came over and took her in his arms. "How about a walk on the beach. We haven't done that in a while."

"That sounds good, then I'll order a pizza."

CHAPTER 7

It doesn't seem real, thought Ally. Everyone is dressed in black. There are baskets and sprays of flowers all over the church. There are memorial standees of Rachel and Evan. Janet and Evan's mom went together to plan the setting.

When she and Neal arrived, Janet told Ally about using a funeral planner, just as she would have a wedding planner. She broke down several times, sobbing uncontrollably. Ally wondered if she could get through the funeral. Their mother arrived last evening with Craig. They are going to stay at Janet's, while Ally and Neal opted for a hotel.

The music had started playing, and everyone was drifting in from the various doors of this enormous church. They decided to hold the funeral services together at Rachel's church, but later that evening, there would be a separate Mass for Evan at their Catholic church. Janet and Adam plan to attend, but the rest of the family does not. Janet arranged a luncheon at a restaurant they frequented. The owners, who were friends of theirs, closed the restaurant for the afternoon to accommodate the family's needs.

The beautiful tune, *"On Eagle's Wings,"* was being played by the pianist. It was time for the family to enter. Evan's mother, Marilyn, entered with Evan's twin, Eric. Adam, Janet, Justin, and Ellen went first, followed by their mother and Craig. Ally and Neal followed, then Adam's brother and his wife. Their sons and their wives were behind them. They were a small clan. Evan's aunts, uncles, and cousins followed. There were several of them. Ally noticed how full it was, with many people of Rachel's age. She was sure they were classmates and friends, having known each other for many years. Young people who had no idea what life would throw at them. She almost pitied them, but then thought, *at least, they are living now.*

The minister stood, greeted everyone, and started with the Lord's Prayer. The words he spoke were comforting; however, there were no words to heal a broken heart.

****

The service was mercifully short. Only two eulogies were given. Justin spoke lovingly about his sister, his only sibling. He spoke of how much he missed her and wished he could see what her children would look like, as he would have wanted her to see his. Janet was audibly shaken when he said that. Ally's heart went out to her sister and Adam—a family, a tribe, forever shattered.

Eric gave the eulogy for his twin brother. He lovingly spoke of how much they shared through the years, and how, after their father died, they made a promise to each other that they would take care of their mom, no matter what. He looked at her and said, "Mom, I will take care of Evan's part, don't worry." There were many sniffles and some crying after he made that statement. Their mother held her head down, but she was visibly shaking.

The post-funeral luncheon was somber, but the food was good. Janet thanked the owners for giving them a place to gather. The funeral director had made sure the two memorial standees were taken to the restaurant. It was surreal seeing the standees again, and Janet could somehow feel Rachel's presence. Yet there was a sense of a veil lifting, allowing them to at least smile again. As noted by Ally, Janet went around to each table and thanked everyone for coming. She had always been the warm, social person that Ally struggled to be. Their mom taught them proper manners, of course, but she especially paid attention to Janet. Ally always wondered why. She had speculated that after her mother had her girl and her boy, she had more or less given up on her. She felt like she was the spare in the tribe. She learned her table manners by watching others. Being the youngest had its advantages, but sometimes she ponders what it would have been like to be the oldest, the apple of her parents' eye, just for a little while.

Later, after Adam and Janet left to go to Evan's Mass, she and Neal rode around Houston, looking at the sights. It was an old city, showing its age. She had heard that homelessness was a problem, and it was evident. There were several tents under overpasses. She wondered how much of it was mental health and veterans with PTSD. Her nursing career saw many homeless people come in with issues that were very simple to address, if only they had access to money or someone to care for them. A lot of it was malnutrition, but many of them were so hooked on drugs that they would rather get a fix than eat. *So sad*, she always thought.

"Want to get a burger?" asked Neal.

"Sure, whatever you want. I don't have an appetite."

They stopped at a place called The Beavers. "I wonder if Jerry Mathers owns it," said Neal.

They got a Mexican hamburger, steak fries, and colas.

On the way home, Ally said, "I am going to do my DNA kit. Have I told you that yet? I can't remember."

"You mentioned it on the plane when we flew back home. I don't think you got around to ordering it."

"Well, I'm going to when we get back. No time like the present. Do you want to do yours?"

"I don't think so. I'm a little leery, but you go ahead. I might change my mind."

When they arrived back at Janet's, they were home from the Mass.

"How was it?" asked Ally.

"Extremely sad. All of Evan's extended family was there. The church was full. I took communion because I felt I had to for Evan. Adam couldn't bring himself to do it. He's having a tough time with all of this, Ally. Much harder than I thought. He was trying to hold it together for me, which I appreciated, but I can see how badly he is hurting. It will take some time."

"Yes, it will," said Neal. "We can stay as long as you need us."

"Yes, we can," echoed Ally.

"That's okay. We will be fine. Mother needs to get back, so she and Craig will stay one more day before leaving. Perhaps y'all need to get home, too. You have done so much for us." Janet hugged both of them.

"I am only a phone call away, okay?" Ally said with tears running down her cheeks.

"I know."

****

Ally logged on to her computer before going to bed and ordered a DNA kit from GEN-match. She had researched it beforehand and knew it was one of the websites that allowed law enforcement to use it to solve crimes. She had always wanted to be a supporter of them, so it felt like the right fit. After paying the fee, they were told the item would be delivered within five days, so they should be home by then.

"I ordered it!"

Neal was on his iPad in bed. "That's good. When will you get it?"

"In about five days."

CHAPTER
8

Two days later, Ally and Neal arrived at the Myrtle Beach airport around five in the afternoon. They decided not to bother Mary with picking them up, since she had already done so much. They got an Uber, and it didn't cost as much as Neal had expected. He commented to Ally, once they were home, that they should maybe do that in the future. "It would be easier on everyone."

Ally nodded in agreement as she stripped out of her clothes and hit the shower. Afterward, she came out in her fluffy robe, which Neal had given her for last Christmas, and got herself a glass of Chardonnay.

She plopped on the sofa and declared, "I am finally tired of travelling. I'm ready to go back to work."

Neal laughed, "Here is the package you were anxious to get."

"Just put it on the bar. I'll take care of it in the morning," Ally told him.

She heard it plop on the counter. "Join me in having some wine," she called out.

"Just about to do that. Give me a minute."

Neal came out of the bedroom wearing only his boxer shorts. He poured himself a glass of wine and came to sit beside her. She put her feet in his lap, and he started massaging them.

"Oh, that feels so good."

"I can make something else feel good, too."

"Maybe wait for morning sex?"

"I was thinking the same thing," he chuckled.

****

The next morning, Ally made them eggs and toast. When Neal came out into the kitchen, she said, "I need to grocery shop today."

"I can help you with that. You need to get Lucky, don't forget," he winked at her.'

She playfully stuck her tongue out and said, "Like I would forget my baby."

She started a grocery list while they were eating. Her phone rang, and she saw it was Gene.

"Hi, what's up, early bird?"

"You're back?" he asked hopefully.

"Yes, last night. I was going to call you this morning."

"We could use you tonight. Can you be available?"

Ally knew he wouldn't ask unless he was really in need. "Of course. Have Sarah text me the details. What time?"

Event starts at six, but you know you'll need to be there by five. Thanks, Ally. Looking forward to seeing you tonight."

"Thanks, Gene. I appreciate your understanding during this time." She hung up.

Neal said, "You got your wish."

She looked at him quizzically. "You said last night that you were ready to go back to work, remember?"

"Now that you mention it, yeah."

She called Mary and said she would come over this morning if that were okay. "Sure, what time?"

"Ten?"

"Yes, see you then."

She saw a text on her phone. It read, Meadowcreek Country Club, wedding reception. An older couple, approximately a hundred people. Only you and Billy, a new hire. Sorry, Eliza on vacay. Sorry about your niece. Talk soon. Be there by 5. Sarah.

"I got my marching orders." She turned her phone so Neal could read the text.

"Sarah is not one to mince words," he said.

She walked over to him and kissed his cheek. Sorry, no morning sex. How about mid-morning?"

"How about afternoon delight?" he asked.

She threw her head back and said, "I'll think about it.' He patted her rear end as she walked off.

****

Her trip to Mary's was very quick. She knew she needed to check on her house, but didn't think she had time. She would want to give it a good cleaning if she stopped, and she knew she had no time for that today. She passed it on her way to Mary's, and it looked okay.

She knocked on Mary's bright blue door once, but then let herself in. She saw Lucky slithering down the hallway, but when he saw her, he headed back. He was twisting himself through her legs when Mary ran up to her. She hugged her and asked her to sit down so they could talk.

"It has been so long since I've seen you, except for the car ride. But we won't count that."

"I know. Usually, I would rattle on about the trip, but it seems like a lifetime ago. We had a great trip; the weather was perfect, and we met many nice people from all over the world. There was a lovely couple from New Zealand we hung around with. I got their email, so we may take them up on their offer to host us. I didn't think at the time we would, but with everything that has gone on, I'm rethinking my priorities."

"That's so interesting. What was your favorite tourist place?"

"Hard to say, but if I had to pick one, it would be Venice. It is so different. A city on water, so unusual, but it was very touristy. Not someplace I care to live; however, Tuscany was a place I could live.

It was so tranquil, and the people were very engaging. The food and wine were to die for; I would go back in a heartbeat. You'll have to go next time."

"I would love to go. Roger's health is not the best, as you know. I'm not going to plan anything until he's feeling better."

"I know, I'm sorry. He'll get better."

"I hope you're right."

Roger was Mary's boyfriend. He was a widower whom she met at church. They have all had dinner together a few times and have found him a lovely man and a good fit for Mary.

"I have a gig tonight. A wedding reception," said Ally.

"Good, getting back into things. Where is it?"

"Meadow Creek, only around a hundred people, so it shouldn't be too crazy. Anyway, I'd better gather Lucky and get going. Let's have lunch in a few days. I need to grocery shop today. The cupboards are bare."

Mary went to get Lucky's carrier and the bag of cat food.

Ally hugged her after putting Lucky in the car. "I'll call you tomorrow, and we'll plan a day to do lunch."

"Sounds good. Be careful."

****

When Ally got home, she saw the note Neal left: *Gone to the store, be back soon.*

"Okay, Lucky, it's just you and me for a while." She picked him up and went out to the sunporch. She wanted to hug him, at least until he demanded to be put down. It was only for a few seconds, then he insisted on getting down. He walked around for a while, then settled on the window seat for a nap.

Meanwhile, Ally thought about her sister and brother-in-law and how they were adjusting to their new reality. The pain must be unbearable. She couldn't imagine. She also thought about her mother and made a mental note to call her later today. She then remembered the kit that came yesterday and went to the kitchen to retrieve it. She had to read through the instructions before opening the packages.

They were very explicit, with diagrams for each process. After she was done, she grabbed her grocery list. She called Neal to find out which store he went to.

"Hello, checking up on me?" asked Neal.

"Do I need to be?"

"No, just kidding. Guess that wasn't too nice."

"Which store did you go to?" asked Ally.

"Home Depot. I needed to get the hardware to repair the screen door. When I arrived, I saw a friend from Raleigh, and we have been talking ever since. I'm sorry, time got away from me."

"I don't mind, just wanted to make sure you didn't go to the grocery store. I'm going to leave in a few minutes to go to Publix. Anything you need?"

"I don't think so, but now that I think about it, pick up a plain creamer. I don't like those artificial-tasting ones."

"Okay, creamer it is. I'll see you later."

"Love you."

"Me too, you," said Ally.

She and Neal had been discussing the benefits of eliminating artificial colors and chemicals. She guessed he was serious, so she planned to shop accordingly.

CHAPTER
9

Ally and Neal had just returned from a walk on the beach and stopped at their mailbox. Neal handed her an envelope.

Ally saw the return address and got excited. "It's from GEN-match."

"So you'll find out who you're related to. Hope there aren't any surprises," Neal chuckled.

She sat down at the kitchen table and opened the envelope. It said she could visit their website, enter her email, then enter the special code they provided. Then she would set up her account and see the report. After all that, she pulled up the report and began reading it. Since her parents hadn't submitted their test, she wasn't listed. Her sister was listed because she uploaded to the same site. She also saw her nephew. Then there was a person listed whom she didn't know, but she had a 51% match with him. It was a male match, and the stated parent was paternal.

"Huh, this is strange. Neal, come look at this."

Neal was looking over her shoulder at the results.

"What does that mean?" he asked.

"I don't know. It appears my DNA is linked to someone I don't even know. How can this person be a parent when I don't know him?"

"It's been a long time since I studied all of this in school, but basically, I believe it means he would be your parent."

"It has to be wrong. How could that be so screwed up? I'm going to see if there is a number to call."

It took her a while to find a customer service number and even longer to get through, but finally she got to a real person who identified herself as Lilly.

"Hello, Lilly? This is Ally Malcom-Smith. I sent my sample saliva to GEN-match and just got my results, and there has to be a mistake."

"Give me the account number on your letter, please."

Ally read the number to her and waited.

"It appears to be a match to you, Mrs. Smith. I could submit an inquiry, which will then undergo a Quality Control process. It will take about four to six weeks. Do you want me to do that?"

"Yes, please. Will someone call me?"

"You should receive a letter telling you what was found. If you still need to call, there will be a number on the letter."

"Does this happen often, I mean, a mistake?"

"We don't know yet that it is a mistake, but yes, I do get these calls quite often. People often discover that they have relatives that they had no idea about."

Ally, in shock, said, "Okay, thank you."

"I will give you a confirmation number about the inquiry. One moment, please."

Lilly came back on the phone and gave Ally the number. Ally hung up and told Neal what she found out.

"My head is spinning. What do I do? This cannot be real."

"You have to wait until they get back in touch. Things happen, darling. You know it's not correct, so they will figure it out and make things right."

"I hope you're right."

****

Ally went to her gig that night, a birthday party for a ninety-nine-year-old man. The family surprised him, and the look on his face showed his surprise. The party was at a gorgeous beach house that his large Italian family rented for vacation. Since he had difficulty walking, his son helped him, but he remained in a wheelchair most of the time. Ally thought of her father and wondered if he would reach this age. She knew that with his Alzheimer's getting worse, it was doubtful.

Her mind went to the GEN-match report, and she got depressed thinking about it. What if? She wondered if she wasn't his child. Was she adopted? She had all of these thoughts going through her head, and she knew she had to snap out of it to get through this night.

They set up several large tables on the deck, along with a large kitchen island and a large round dining table. Some people had to stand, well-wishers they knew from vacationing in this area for many years. They didn't seem to mind. She served them drinks while Billy brought out the appetizer, shrimp cocktails. Afterwards, dinner was served, which included lobster tails and steak. Everyone seemed to be pleased with the food choices.

Billy was doing very well. It was a summer job for him; he goes back to NC State in the fall. They worked well together. She missed Eliza, but now that they were well-trained, they rarely worked together during the high season. Gene relied on his experienced staff to be on-site, and he often had two or three gigs on weekends during the summer months.

She got home around ten. The family had games planned for after dinner and wanted the catering staff out by nine. She crawled into bed next to Neal and tapped him on the shoulder, "Surprise."

He had not been asleep for long and was happy to see her. He rolled over to face her, then kissed her deeply.

"Ummm, that was nice, let's do more foreplay in the future, Mr. Smith."

"Foreplay? I'm just getting started," he said as he pulled her closer to him and fondled her breast.

After they finished making love, Ally realized she was starving. "I never ate tonight. I'll be right back."

She came in a few minutes later with a peanut butter-and-pickle sandwich.

"My favorite go-to food," she said.

"I know, I love them, too."

She turned on the wall TV and watched a rerun of *Bull.*

"I don't know why they took this show off the air; it was one of my favorites," said Neal.

"I think the star was ready to stop. They should have let Marissa take over, in my opinion," said Ally.

****

The next morning, they slept later than usual. Ally was drained of energy after the last two weeks.

"I have a lunch date with Mary today. I hope you didn't plan anything. I forgot to mention it to you. I have been so busy, I haven't spent enough time with her. Roger isn't doing well."

"No worries, have fun. Ask about Roger and let me know. I should see him. I'm going to work on paying bills today."

"You're not using your accountant to do that anymore?"

"I told him I would take it over after we got back from our honeymoon. He had everything caught up and even paid ahead until now. I don't have much else to do, so I thought I should do it."

"When are you going to write that great novel you've always been eager to write?"

"I don't know," he said with his forefinger on his chin. "Maybe when I have an idea of something to write about."

"You mean, I haven't given you enough yet?" she laughed.

"Almost, but need a few more mysteries. Speaking of mysteries, have you told Mary about your report or anyone else?"

"Nope, not going to until I know more."

At noon, Ally picked Mary up, and they headed to their favorite lunch spot. "I never get tired of this place," said Mary.

"How is Roger? Neal wanted me to make sure I asked you. I think he wants to go see him."

"He is better. His doctor advised him to stay out of the heat because it was too strenuous for his heart. He takes a couple of heart pills, and one of them causes him to flush if he gets too hot. He has what he calls 'spells,'" she laughed. "Like an old woman."

"Good, hopefully he will heed the doctor's advice."

"Speaking of doctors, is Neal missing work?"

"Doesn't seem to be."

Their number was called to pick up their food. "I'll get it," Ally said as she stood up.

After she sat back down, she said, "He decided to start paying his bills. He is busy today setting everything up the way he likes so that it will be easier. He is organized and conscientious about it."

"So, you are going to keep your accounts separate? I'm sorry, I shouldn't have asked, none of my business."

"No, that's okay. I don't mind. Yes, I want to stay independent. We may combine when we get older. The important things we have taken care of are our wills. He has named me the beneficiary of his investments. His son is provided for in his will with a substantial inheritance. Since I don't have any children and only one nephew, now that Rachel has passed, I will add him as a beneficiary to my will and leave him part of my estate. Most of it will go to the Doe project for DNA matching."

"That's good of you, Ally."

"It's what I am most passionate about, so why not?" She was enjoying her chicken salad.

"How about some consignment shopping today?" asked Ally.

"You're not working today?"

"No, day off. Nothing until Saturday."

"Okay, let's," said Mary.

They spent the rest of the afternoon visiting and browsing through the consignment shops in the area. Ally bought a sundress for beach walks, and Mary found a couple of pillows for her front porch.

"The traffic keeps getting worse," commented Ally as she pulled up to a light.

"Tourist. Imagine a tourist in a tourist town," Mary laughed.

Ally dropped Mary off at her house, then went back down the street and stopped at her place. She doesn't know what to do with it. Technically, it still belongs to her mother, but she has too much on her plate these days to make any decisions.

She made sure there were no disturbances inside the house. It smelled a little musty, having been closed up for about 3 months. She opened a window in the back bedroom, the one that doesn't face the street. She hoped it would help it air out. She checked the refrigerator to make sure there were no problems with it or any food they had overlooked. Everything looked fine. Then she double checked the waste baskets, and they were okay. She was satisfied that it was secure, except for the window she had just opened, and left, locking the deadbolt.

She made a mental note to return in a day or two to ensure nothing had been disturbed. She planned to have Neal accompany her so he could inspect the appliances and check for leaks. The water was still on in the house, but they had turned off the valves to the toilets and the washer before leaving for their honeymoon. She wants them to stay off for now.

On her drive home, she couldn't help but reminisce about when she moved in, met Mary, and then Neal. This house held many memories for her. She smiled when she thought of them and was grateful to her family for all they had done to help her after her escape from New York.

****

When she arrived home, Neal was hunched over the kitchen table, looking at his computer.

"Why don't you do that in your office, darling?"

"I just wanted to spread everything out, and there was more light and room out here. I'll put it away before dinner."

"Don't worry about that. It's a nice day, and we can eat out in the sunroom. It shouldn't be too hot. I'll go put them down now."

"Okay, if that is alright with you. This job is taking me longer than I thought."

"How so?"

"I'm having to set up everything in my name and get new pass-words. Bob warned me it would take a while, and he was right."

"Don't drive yourself crazy. Take a break."

"Good idea, I'll go to the mailbox."

As he walked back up the drive, Ally happened to look out the window and saw him looking down at the mail. He spent an unusual amount of time staring at it, thought Ally. She had a feeling it was her reply from GEN-match.

"I have a piece of mail for you, Ally," he said as he walked into the mudroom.

"Is it what I think it is?"

"I believe so. Here."

She took the letter and quickly opened it. After unfolding the one page, she skimmed it until she got to the part which said, 'No error has been detected after checking our records. If you would like to submit another sample, please order the kit online and reference this number: A389251.'

Ally dropped the letter, and Neal heard her gasp. He ran over, picked it up, and also scanned it. He could see that she was distraught.

"You need to resubmit, Ally. You must be positive before pursuing this. It states here that using this number would expedite your next sample. I'll go online and order it for you, okay?"

She nodded, but couldn't speak. She could only think about all the time she spent with her father. How could he not be her birth father? What happened? She knew she wasn't adopted because she had matched with her sister, but was it a correct percentage? Now she wondered what the rate of siblings not from the same parentage, only part, would be. She visualized the times her father took her to school and picked her up. He was so good to her. He even helped her with her homework, even when he was tired. Nothing was more import-ant than his children. He was a warm, loving parent. Her mother was paradoxical. Ally felt she never had a close relationship with her mother, at least not as close as Janet had. She had felt a closeness with her father, though. She loved her mother, but something always felt off in their relationship.

"Okay, it's on its way," said Neal.

She looked up like she didn't know what he was talking about.

"Are you okay, Ally? You don't look well."

She started crying. "I don't know anything anymore. Is the sky blue? Is the grass green? How would I know? If my father is not my father, then who is this man...Hugh Fitz something, I don't even remember because I thought it was wrong."

"C'mon."

He stood her up and walked her to the bedroom, removed her shoes, and pulled back the covers. He laid her back on her pillow and pulled the covers up.

"Just try to rest. We'll talk about this later. You're too upset. I love you." He kissed the top of her head.

CHAPTER
10

"What should I do?"

"Darling, I wish I could advise you. I've never known any-one who has been in this situation. We'll have the new kit in a couple of days. I paid extra for shipping. Don't you want to resend the sample and see if the results are different? You can't go questioning your mother without the second test completed," said Neal.

"I could ask her, but I won't. You're right, but I am going to look up that person and see if I can find anything about him."

"I don't blame you. I would probably do the same. Please don't make any calls without talking with me, okay?"

"Okay."

Ally picked up her laptop and sat on the sofa. The sun was set-ting behind her, so her light was getting dim. She turned on the table lamp. She had been noticing lately that she was having difficulty with close-up reading. Presbyopia, they call it.

"I think I need to go to the eye doctor, Neal."

"I know a good one down here. He is highly recommended."

"Great, would you write his name on the pad there in the kitchen, and I'll look him up tomorrow."

She signed onto the GEN-match site and found her report. The name was William Brian Fitzgerald. She had the name completely wrong. It seemed she had seen it as Hugh something, but again, it's probably her eyes, she thought.

She Googled the name and found too many results, including other variations. She didn't have time for that. She went to Facebook, entered the name, and the same thing happened. She wondered if mentioning their hometown in New York would help her make better progress. She put in his name and town: Eldridge, and she got better results.

A profile for Bill Fitzgerald appeared. His picture showed an older man with a round face and a neatly groomed, white beard. He was with a woman, probably his wife. She wore glasses and had a pretty face with short, reddish-blonde hair that was very stylish. His profile stated that he was retired. Previously, he served as the Chief of the Eldridge Police Department.

"Neal, come here," she shouted.

He came running from the bedroom. "Oh, good, I thought you were hurt. You scared me to death."

"Come see this," she said.

He looked over her shoulder and observed the Facebook page, reading Bill's profile. "Do you think this could be the same person?"

"I know it is."

"How do you know?"

"I remember his face. I think he may have come to our school, and I may have seen him at our house. He looks familiar."

"Oh, sweetie. I'm so sorry. I still think you should retake the test before asking your mother. She isn't in a good place right now."

"I will wait, but it's going to take all of the willpower I have."

****

The next morning, Ally decided to take a walk on the beach. She got up before Neal because she wanted to go alone. The sun was cresting in the east, and there were only a few people out at this hour. It had been too long since she had walked in solitude. She needed to think through everything she had learned about her past and her potential destiny.

She distinctly remembered 'Chief Bill', as they called him. He was a frequent visitor to their home. She doesn't remember if he was married; he never had a woman with him. She always assumed they knew him well, since her father was a pharmacist and owned his own store. It made sense that he would want to know the police officers in town, especially the chief.

She had visions of her mother inviting him in whenever he showed up. It never occurred to her young, innocent mind that there could be something between them. Now that she was older and more mature, she was aware that women have affairs almost as much as men. What happens between consensual adults is their business, but she had a hard time with the thought that her mother may have strayed from her marriage. Her mother never worked outside the home and had time on her hands; was she bored, she wondered. Her mother had come from old money and had a Trust Fund left by her great-grandfather. She wasn't one to spend lavishly. They lived in a nice neighborhood, and her father provided well for them. They ensured that money was set aside for their children's education. Money was never a topic of conversation in their home.

She knew she was an 'oops' baby, at least she suspected once she was old enough to understand reproduction. Her mother was in her late thirties when she was born. Her father was around the same age. She never remembered or cared about the year they were born. It never interested her until now. She realized she had a lot to figure out.

She needed to call her sister to see how she was doing. She would be careful and hoped Janet wouldn't ask her about her DNA test. It's doubtful she will, since she has too much else on her mind. She also needed to call her mother, but she couldn't bring herself to do that now.

It just dawned on her that she didn't take her phone. Neal was going to get up and wonder what had happened to her. He was being extra vigilant lately around her. She guessed he was worried about her mental state. She decided she needed to get back.

She ran to the house and, as she approached the walkway, saw Neal on the back deck, binoculars in hand, looking for her. She started waving at him. He saw her and waved back.

"I'm sorry, I forgot to take my phone and then realized you would worry, so I ran back. It was a great morning for a walk."

"It looks like it would be. You need some alone time, I understand." He reached for her hand and walked inside with her.

"Do you want me to go to the bagel store?"

"Not for me, but you go if you want to. I will eat my muesli and fruit. I need to get off bread and pasta for a while."

"Yeah, I should too. I'll have coffee and make myself some scrambled eggs," he said.

"Just sit, I'll get your eggs for you. I can multitask. After all, I was a nurse," she laughed.

"Thanks, I'll take you up on that. He got his coffee and sat on a barstool while she was busy in the kitchen."

"I need to finish up my financial work, so I'll be busy with that this morning. Is there anything you want to do later?"

"No, I need to do some cleaning and go check on the house. Did you feed Lucky?" she asked.

"Yes, all taken care of. He's on the sun porch."

After she gave Neal his eggs, she went out to the porch to check on Lucky. He was in the window seat, his favorite place. She petted him, and he looked up at her and meowed. "I think it is time for your vet check-up. I'll call today and make you an appointment."

She scrolled through her emails on her phone while she was eating and found the vet reminder. She called, and they made an appointment for the next day.

"I'm taking Lucky in for his check-up tomorrow. Want to come?" she asked Neal.

"Maybe, let me see what tomorrow brings."

CHAPTER 11

Ally was making a salad for dinner. She had invited Mary over for dinner. Roger still wasn't feeling well, and she felt Mary could use an evening out, away from the responsibility of Roger's needs.

She heard Neal's BMW drive into the carport. He had gone to the local accountant because he was deeply involved in one of his accounts and had given up trying to find the error in the numbers. It was frustrating him, so she suggested the accountant that Mary used.

"How'd it go?" she cheerily asked him.

"It went," he told her, then went into his office and laid the paperwork on his desk.

When he came out, he told her that the accountant had taken a look but would need a day or two to conduct the "autopsy" on his books.

"That doesn't sound good."

"I've got ten thousand dollars missing. I don't like leaving money on the table, as you know."

"I know. He will find the mistake, don't worry. Chardonnay or something stronger?"

"Stronger. I'm going to get the mail," he told her.

She made him a scotch and poured herself a glass of wine.

When he returned, he handed her the envelope they both dreaded.

"Should I open it now, before Mary gets here?" she asked him.

"Up to you. It might upset you too much."

"Yeah, but I'll go crazy not knowing, she'd be the first one I would tell anyway."

She opened the envelope, dreading the results, and, as expected, it contained a second code for her to look up online. She opened the website, entered the new code, and the report appeared. The same name stared at her: William Brian Fitzgerald. She dropped her forehead into her open hands. Neal came up behind her and massaged her neck. "I'm sorry."

"I need to finish up dinner before Mary gets here. I'd better get everything ready, so I can sit down and talk with her."

After she had the steaks ready to grill and the asparagus cleaned and in the large pan she uses for cooking, she poured another glass of wine and sat on the front porch, waiting for Mary. They had laughed and cried together a lot since they met three years ago. She knew she could count on her for advice.

Mary pulled her car into the driveway and stepped out. She wore a casual red knit dress, a short white jacket, and white sandals. She always dressed so conservatively. She spotted Ally on the porch and waved to her. As she walked up the steps, she commented on the geraniums. "At least the deer haven't gotten yours."

"So far."

She hugged Mary and said, I have something to tell you and need your advice. What do you want to drink?"

"Do I need something harder than wine?"

"No, I don't think so."

"Then I'll have what you're having."

"I'll get it, have a seat."

She came back out with Mary's wine and sat in the chair next to hers. These were a pair she found at a yard sale last year, and she remembered them painting together.

"You know, with Rachel's death, they did a DNA test on Janet and Adam when the car was located. They had to use DNA to confirm the results at autopsy."

"Yes, I remember you telling me. DNA has revolutionized how we identify people today. I guess they don't bother getting dental records."

"I don't know about that, but that's not what I'm about to tell you."

"Well, what is it?"

"I decided to check my DNA just for fun. I got the results back several weeks ago, but then had them repeated."

"Why would you have to do that?" asked Mary.

"Because I didn't believe my results. It showed my father to be someone else, not John Malcom."

Mary stared at Ally, and her eyes narrowed with concern and confusion.

"You weren't adopted or anything. I thought you were the baby of the family."

"I was their third and final child. That was why I had the test repeated. I used a website called GEN-match because their site allows law enforcement to check for matches for the DNA of bodies they find and to help find criminals."

"Oh, okay."

"I didn't expect my parents to be listed. I don't think either of them has ever entered their DNA into an ancestry site. It wasn't a 'thing' until a few years ago. They aren't into doing genealogy."

"Have you spoken with your mother?"

"Heaven's no, I just got the second result this afternoon. I need your advice on what to do."

"I don't know, Ally. Maybe talk with your sister?"

"No, she has too much on her plate. I can't do that to her now. This is something I need to discuss with my mother. I suppose I'll visit them. I need to anyway because my father is going downhill. He wasn't able to go to Rachel's funeral, and he hasn't even been told about the accident."

"I remember you telling me that. I am so sorry. You hear about these things happening, but I haven't known anyone who's had them happen to them. It's usually on one of those Dateline shows or some other show about family drama. For sure, it is a delicate subject. What does Neal say?"

"The same. He doesn't know what I should do either. Let's go inside. I'll get him to put the steaks on, and maybe we can discuss it over dinner."

They had an excellent meal, thanks to Neal's expertise on the steaks. Ally didn't have an appetite until she started eating and realized she hadn't had lunch. Her system hasn't been right since they got back from Italy, with all of the traveling due to Rachel's accident, subsequent death, and funeral. She had been trying to get back to her old eating habits and see a drop in her weight. She gained five pounds in Italy from eating pasta and drinking wine. Still, she wouldn't have traded the time with Neal for anything. The countryside of Tuscany was so peaceful, yet she also loved the hustle and bustle of Florence and Milan. She purchased a leather handbag in Florence. That was her splurge item. She tried to get Neal to get a new leather jacket, but he resisted. "I have enough leather to last a lifetime. Besides, where would I wear it?" he asked her. He was right, they didn't get much cold weather where they lived. It was impractical.

"Have you found the man you believe to be your father on Facebook?" Mary interrupted Ally's thoughts.

"I have, at least I think it is him. I could be wrong. I'll show you after dinner."

"Ally, you and I need to go to Florida so you can discuss all of this with your mother," Neal told her.

"Yes, I know. It is just too much. All of this right on the heels of Rachel's death. How will I broach the subject?"

"That's a good question," said Mary. "You will know when the time is right," she reassured her.

Once they finished their meal, Neal offered to clean up so they could check Facebook.

"Thank you, darling," Ally told him.

She pulled her laptop up on the coffee table and opened her Facebook account. She entered his name, and it populated immediately, since he had been a recent search.

"He is a nice-looking man," said Mary.

"That's not what I am looking for in a father," Ally reminded her.

"I know, it is just an uncomfortable subject. I don't believe this can be real. Your mother surely would know if she had an affair with this man."

"That's what I'm afraid of. My father's mind is so far gone that I hope he doesn't hear any of our conversation. But, what if he knew about it and they never told me?"

"Have you thought about discussing any of this with a therapist before you bring it up with your mother?" asked Mary.

"That isn't a bad idea," Neal added.

"That is not a bad idea at all. I need professional help. It is too sensitive a subject, and there are no easy answers."

"Neal, do you know of anyone?"

"Let me think about it. I believe I had a roommate in college who was pursuing a career in psychiatry. Even if he is retired, he may be able to refer you to someone."

"Sounds like a plan, thank you."

CHAPTER 12

Ally contacted a woman recommended by Neal's friend. She was a therapist who specialized in family issues, and one she had handled before was relatives finding half siblings and parents they knew nothing about. She had a Zoom call scheduled for four o'clock that same day.

She was nervous and made herself a drink in advance. Typically, she had white wine, but for this call, she made herself a scotch and water. The woman's name was Brittany Sebring, and she was located in Charlotte. She told Ally that she had many clients across the country and that using Zoom had revolutionized her business. She no longer had to pay office overhead, so her fees had been significantly reduced. Her clients had picked up considerably, and she did her own scheduling. It was a win-win for everyone, she told her.

Neal left the house so she could have privacy. He was curious, of course, but he knew she would tell him everything when he returned.

She clicked the link on her computer one minute before the appointment. Dr. Sebring was already online. She formally introduced herself to Ally and broke the ice by asking Ally a few informal questions. Then she broached the subject of discovering she had a different name in her family tree than she expected.

"How did you feel when you saw the name?"

"Shocked, of course. I wasn't sure what it meant. My husband encouraged me to have them check on their end for an error, which I did. When it came back with no error, I requested another kit, which they suggested and even prioritized. Once I received that result, I was even more confused. The questions were rolling around in my head like a pinball in one of those old-time machines you played at arcades."

"What type of questions. Could you elaborate?"

"How, why, when, did my mother have an affair? I even wondered at one point if they could be swingers! Isn't that ridiculous?"

"No, I don't think that is ridiculous. Ally, people have many secrets. Some of them want to share, and others are too ashamed. I think yours is of the latter. What do I mean by that? I think your mother may have had an affair and gotten pregnant with you, but didn't tell your father, therefore never told you. She probably never in a million years thought it would be discovered. DNA was not a thing back then. Well, it was being discussed, but never to the extent that it has become used today. Another thing, which I am hesitant to mention, but I think it could be a possibility, is that she may have been raped."

"Raped? Really?"

"It happens, Ally. I've seen it more times than I want to think about. Women often do not report for various reasons. Shame, guilt. She may have told your father, and they agreed not to say anything, then when she found out she was pregnant, she just hoped that your father had impregnated her. It is a fifty-fifty deal. She may have prayed or kept her fingers crossed. There are many possibilities."

"What should I do? Anything?"

"If you feel you need to know, then plan to talk with her, but do it very gently. If she shuts you down, then I would advise letting her be. She may come back after she has had time to think it over and decide she owes you an explanation. You said your father had Alzheimer's, I believe?"

"Yes, that is correct."

"This is a precarious time for your mother. I know you want to know, but I think you should give it more thought and maybe not bring it up now. But if you feel you must, do it in the gentlest way possible."

"Okay, I understand. I will discuss it with my husband, and we'll decide. I thank you for your time."

"You're welcome. I wish you luck, and don't hesitate to get in touch with me again if you have more questions or want to talk."

****

"I'm home," Ally called out as she walked in the back door." She walked to the window seat in the sun porch and picked up Lucky. "How's my boy?" she squeezed him tight.

She had driven over to check her beach house and to see Mary. They enjoyed a lemonade on her front porch. Ally always enjoyed Mary's company and wanted to tell her about her call with the psychiatrist.

"So, she thinks you should put it aside for a while? What do you want to do?"

"I want to confront my mother. I have thought it over, and even though my dad, the one I thought was my dad, has Alzheimer's, I think she owes me an explanation. My dad could be in the same condition for many years. It's a strange disease and moves slowly."

"Are you going to Florida?"

"I have to, Mary. It's not something I can ask her on the phone. What would you do?"

"I've been thinking about it, and I honestly don't know. When you grow up under the auspices of one belief, that being, your mom is your mom and your dad is your dad, you don't expect to have that rug pulled out from under you, especially at this age and these circumstances. What if you had found out after they passed? You would have never had the chance to ask her."

"You're right. I hadn't thought about that. Even more urgent in my opinion."

"You plan to go to Florida alone?"

"I think I should go alone. Neal offered and would go if I asked, but this is something so personal, I don't feel right bringing him into it. I want to have an open and honest discussion with my mother. Besides, we have been gone so much, he needs to get caught up on bills and other things."

After she left Mary's, she stopped at the nearest vegetable stand and got some ingredients for a salad. Their tomatoes were so good.

When she arrived home, she wondered where Neal was, but decided to start dinner, assuming he would be home soon. She put in her earbuds and turned on a podcast on her phone's app. She had missed a lot of them lately, so she had plenty to choose from. She decided to listen to one set in Florida.

She finished the dinner preparation, poured a glass of wine, and sat on the porch with Lucky, still listening to the podcast. Before she knew it, she had lain down and fallen asleep with Lucky on her chest.

"Ally, Ally, wake up," Neal was standing over her. Ally slowly opened her eyes and finally focused on the voice calling her name. She was groggy, but she sat up and realized she had fallen asleep.

"What time is it?" she asked.

Neal glanced at the wall clock and told her it was seven.

"In the morning?"

"No, darling. In the evening. You were so far gone; do you want to go to bed?"

Ally said, "No, I'm okay. I started dinner and will finish getting it ready."

"I'm not sure I have an appetite now," Neal told her, with a deep sigh.

"What do you mean?" asked Ally.

"There is $42,000 missing from my investments."

CHAPTER
13

"What happened?" asked Ally.

"I made the mistake of not paying enough attention to my balances, and someone in my financial planner's office transferred funds, just small amounts over time. He knew he had to cover his tracks, so he made up funds and enriched himself. I was being embezzled for over two years and had no idea."

"How did you figure it out?"

"I set up a Quicken account a few years ago to track my investments, but didn't keep it up as I should have. It's all my fault."

"It's not your fault for losing the money. Just because you didn't keep up a home account, it's your finance planner who is in trouble."

"That's the other thing. After meeting with Alan today, he explained that the employee who embezzled the money had a legitimate reason for needing it. It is wrong, of course. But the young man's daughter has a rare blood disease, and he is drowning in debt. Alan isn't a pushover; he was aware of the man's situation. He feels terrible about it. The mother isn't able to work due to caring for their only child. He bears all the financial responsibility."

"What are you going to do, Neal. I don't think the amount of money is the issue, but you were robbed."

"I know, Ally. Alan has offered to make my account whole. He let the young man go, and he felt sincerely terrible about it, but he knew he wouldn't be able to trust him. I have to decide whether or not to press charges."

"Of course, you have to, right?" asked Ally.

"Do I? Did we not learn anything from Katie, your friend who helped so many people in her short time on this earth?"

"I'm sorry, I guess I didn't think about it that way. You would, of course, because you're innately kind. I'm ashamed of thinking that way."

"Alan told me the man is surrendering his license. Alan has spoken with the Detective who handles financial crimes. Since it is a first offense, he has agreed to go to bat for him and get probation. He will have to get a much lower-paying job, but at least he won't be in prison. He will also have a lien for the amount of money he stole. It is going to hurt him in the long run, but if things go well, his little girl will beat this disease. She does have a chance, unlike some diseases."

"That's great, darling." She leaned over and kissed him.

"Ready to eat?" she asked.

"Yes, I do think I have an appetite."

"Give me a few. Want a drink?"

"Yes, but something harder, scotch."

"Coming up," said Ally.

After dinner, Ally looked up flights for Tampa. She found one out of Myrtle Beach on an airline called Allianz. She called her mom, and she picked up on the second ring.

"Hello, Ally. Good to hear from you."

Ally knew that was code for "why haven't you called in a while?" She decided not to take the bait.

"How are you and Daddy doing?"

"We're okay. Your father has his good days, and we can go out to lunch or shopping. Most days, though, he spends in front of the TV. He was never a TV watcher, until recently."

"Yeah, I remember. He would rather read. I admired that and wondered if I got my love of reading from him."

"Maybe," Gloria said, "but I'm a good reader, too. You may have gotten it from me."

A test. She took the bait and failed.

Ally told her mom she wanted to come for a visit.

"That's great, I look forward to seeing you and Neal under better circumstances."

"Neal isn't coming with me. Just little 'ole me."

"Oh, okay. Well, I look forward to seeing you."

Another test. She failed, but in a different way. Ally always knew she was treated differently.

"Is there a date I shouldn't come? I am looking up fares as we speak. I can get a flight into Tampa next Tuesday."

"That would be fine. You'll get a car?" asked her mom.

"Yes, I will. I'll be fine. I'll use my phone for the directions. I find it is more reliable."

"Great. I'll tell your father you're coming, although he won't remember. I'm afraid he is failing fast, Ally. I'm glad you're coming."

"Me too. Love you both. I'll call Monday to confirm my flight times, or earlier if you need me to."

"No, that is fine. Monday is good. Talk then. Love you, Ally." She hung up.

She found Neal in his office, looking at the computer. "Catching up, dear?"

"Yeah. I sent Alan an email letting him know that I discussed everything with you and that we have decided, for sure, not to file charges. That is what we decided, right?"

"Yes, of course. Pay it forward. I pray he finds a job to support his family and get his life back on track. What a waste, but I'm hopeful for their daughter," said Ally.

"I just got off the phone with Mom. She is pleased I am coming, but I could tell she would rather you were coming with me."

He laughed. "What can I say, I charm the ladies."

"Let's go to bed, I'm exhausted."

"I'll be there soon. Just want to check my emails and get caught up. What is the name of the computer place you told me about? I need to get another computer or get this one cleaned out."

"Total Computer Solutions. Mike will take care of you."

"I'll call them tomorrow."

"We need to get our wills done, too. Do you want me to look into an attorney here?"

"Why don't we use the same attorney I've had for several years. He did mine after my divorce; I'll give him a call or send an email."

"That is fine with me. I'm going to call Sarah tomorrow and see if I can work this weekend. Since I'm leaving on Tuesday, I'd like to help them out if they need it."

"Sure, no worries. Good idea."

She kissed him on the top of the head and said, I'll wait up."

****

The next morning, Ally arose before Neal. She wanted to get in a beach walk before breakfast. She needed to make use of her hours that day to get organized for her trip. She had been working out in her head how to bring up the subject with her mother. She couldn't just come out and say, 'Did you have an affair?' Well, maybe she could and should, on second thought. Her stomach was in knots just thinking about it.

Neal was so tender last night. She had fallen asleep by the time he came to bed. Her book was lying on her lap, and the light was still on. Lucky was at the end of the bed, curled up asleep. Neal nuzzled her neck and moved her book, turned out her light, and curled up to her back, spooning her. She felt his arousal through her thin gown and turned on her back. He massaged her breasts and felt her wetness. He entered her and began slowly, ending with thrusts which grew rapid. She groaned and, with him using his hands on her breasts, she managed a climax so pleasant that she barely knew it had happened. When he had finished, Neal went to take a shower. She fell back asleep and never heard him again.

She felt great this morning. Her energy had increased every day since they arrived back home. She was so tired from the cruise and the shock of Rachel's death and funeral. Life is great right now. She just wondered what she would learn about her parentage. It was that question mark that was front and center in everything she did.

CHAPTER
14

*A*lly was six years old and about to begin first grade. She would start at the same elementary school as her sister and brother. Her brother was beginning at the middle school this year, and Janet was a Junior in High School. In their family, it was tradition for their father to take them to school on their first day. Janet was driving, so she was exempt this year, she remembered. She had been gifted a car by their grandmother, Harriett. It was a used Oldsmobile Cutlass in burgundy. Janet loved it. She could carry her friends around, and it made her feel so grown-up. She had started working at their family's pharmacy part-time during the summer to earn gas money.

Ally put her clothes out the night before so she would be ready to go the next morning. She decided to wear her light-blue skirt and white blouse, with blue flowers on the collar and cuffs. She had her mother put her hair in a ponytail and tie it with the pretty blue ribbon they had purchased at the fabric store. She had a selection of ribbons to match every outfit. Her hair was blonde and very long. Her mother took her to the salon to have it cut shorter for school, but it was still past her shoulders.

After dropping off Craig at the middle school, they had a short drive to Meadowlark Elementary. She climbed into the front seat after Craig got out of the car. Her dad smiled at her and asked if she was ready.

"I think so. How hard can it be?" asked Ally.

Her dad chuckled, "That's my girl, you are the bravest one I know."

Ally had tears in her eyes as she thought of that moment. She could remember it as clear as the Carolina sky above her. *If only I were his girl*, she thought.

When she got back to the house, Neal was up and drinking his coffee in the kitchen. "I fed Lucky, he was meowing."

"Thanks," she said as she was pouring a cup of coffee. "I'm going to call Three Island in a few minutes to see if they have any jobs for me this coming weekend."

"You mentioned it last night, that's fine."

"Yeah, I remember now. I have so much on my mind, sorry."

Neal walked up and kissed her on the neck. "I'm sorry, I know you are a bit stressed. No worries. How about we go out tonight for dinner and invite Mary and Roger?"

"Great idea. First, let me find out if Sarah needs me."

She dialed her employer, and Sarah answered. "Good morning, Ally. How are you?"

"I'm okay, you?"

"Doing great. We could use you this weekend, if that is why you are calling. Eliza had an emergency and needs Saturday off. We have a wedding in the evening, and the reception starts around seven. One of those destination weddings on the beach. Could you do it?"

"I sure can. Please send me all the details. Anything else?"

"No, not right now, but I will let you know if anything comes up."

"I'm leaving next Tuesday to go visit my parents in Florida, but plan to be back the following Friday. I could be available on Saturday."

"I will put that down. We are more flexible now that we have some college students working. That was a great lead you gave us."

"Thanks, Sarah. Give my love to Gene. Take care."

Sarah was referring to the student Ally met at the local college where she and Mary go to exercise. He was a young man working there to earn money for his college tuition. His name was Nick, and he reminded her of her brother. They talked every time she was in, and she learned that he was abandoned at a young age due to his mother being on drugs. His father had been in prison when he was born, and he was released about five years before, but had not chosen to contact his son. Ally felt sorry for him and took him under her wing. She tipped him five dollars each time she was there. Not too much, so he wouldn't think it was a 'pity' tip. After a while, she asked if he could use another job that paid better and was probably more flexible. She got him an interview with Gene, and he and Sarah loved him. Gene has become a father figure to him, one he never had.

It worked out so well that Nick had referred his friends to Gene, who had a pool of kids to draw from and was never short-staffed. The business expanded and started getting five-star ratings on its website.

Sarah had helped Gene so much with her organizational skills. He became more creative in his menu choices, making Three Island more competitive. He was much more relaxed, even dating from time to time. She was glad he had made contact with some cousins on his mother's side after taking his DNA test. Now he has a family to go to for holidays.

"Guess what?" she asked Neal when he walked in from the carport.

"What?"

"I am free tonight, I'll call Mary."

****

They decided to try a new restaurant in Myrtle Beach. They wanted to make it easier for Roger. He was better but still a bit frail. After being seated, Neal ordered his favorite bottle of Josh Cellars Cabernet.

"Roger, how are you doing?" asked Ally.

"The good news is the pacemaker is working fine. I'm still weak, though. I'm the worst patient, Ally. This recuperation has made me depressed."

Ally knew from her days of nursing that men suffered from depression after any cardiac event. Heart attacks were worse. She wondered if his doctor knew, but it wasn't her place to ask. She made a mental note to say something to Mary later.

"I hope you feel better soon. We miss being with you."

Neal said, "I agree, I'm ready for us to go fishing when you are up to it. Would you like to go out to breakfast sometime? Just you and me?"

"I would love that. It would get me up in the morning."

"I tell you what, let's plan on next Wednesday morning. Ally will be going to Florida on Tuesday, and I could use the company."

"That works, don't think I have anything going on," he said, looking at Mary.

"No, no doctor appointments next week at all," she assured him.

They ordered their dinners and continued catching up on what was happening in their area.

"I'll be glad when tourist season is over," said Mary. "The traffic is unbearable during the day."

"I know, but that is what keeps our taxes low, don't forget," Ally laughed. "A little pain with a lot of gain."

Neal nodded, but he was thinking about the money he lost. It occurred to him that if he had not found the mistake, Alan might never have mentioned it. *Something to check on*, he thought. He planned to bring it up with Ally later. He wondered how many other clients had been embezzled. It wasn't a subject he wanted to broach around their friends.

Once they had paid the check, they made their way through the serpentine route to the front door of the bustling restaurant. Neal tried to pay for everyone, but Roger wouldn't let him. "Another time, maybe," Roger laughed, and they added their respective cards to the check presenters.

Since Roger lived closest to the restaurant, they dropped him off. He invited them in for a nightcap, but they were all tired and politely declined. "Okay, I'll see you on Wednesday, Neal. Early, say seven?"

"Works for me," Neal told him.

Mary waited for the door to close, then said, "Thank you, Neal. You don't know how much Roger needs to get out. It will be so good for him."

"My pleasure, I need it, too."

CHAPTER 15

Neal was driving Ally to the airport for her trip to Florida. He knew she was worried about it because she had not slept well for a couple of nights.

"I still haven't decided how to bring it up to her. I mean, what do you say to your mother when you find out she must have had an affair and never told anyone?"

"You'll know when the time comes. Try not to be so defensive," he suggested.

"That's easy for you to say."

Neither of them spoke for a few minutes, then Neal said, "I'll miss you."

"Me too, you," she smiled at him.

She gave him a hug at the curb and made her way to the baggage check. Although she had a carry-on-size bag, she preferred to check it since she didn't have a layover. She hated having to store a bag overhead and then get it on the other end.

She used the time at the gate to catch up on her reading. She had not been as prolific as she used to be, reading at least one or two books a week. The podcasts she had been listening to had been taking up most of her downtime, but she decided to put them on hold during this trip. She wants to focus solely on her parents and their lives. She heard from her mother last night that her brother Craig and his girlfriend were coming to dinner while she was there. She hoped it wasn't going to be awkward because her main goal was to hash out her paternity. She was certain her brother and sister were unaware of what she knew.

****

After collecting her bag, she went to the Avis rental kiosk and inserted her credit card. She received a ticket upon delivery of her car. It took her a few minutes to figure out the rental cars were on the opposite side of the terminal. She was glad she wore her HOKA's because it was a long walk. She had not been working out as regularly as she had before her honeymoon, and she was starting to feel the effects—another priority she needed to get back to when she returned.

It wasn't long before a silver Kia pulled up with an Avis sign on the dashboard. She presented her ticket and her license, which he entered into the handheld device. She signed, then got in the car and adjusted the seat and mirrors. The first thing she needed to do was enter her parents' address into her Google Maps. After that was done, she pulled out and headed east.

The trip was uneventful, and she arrived in Bartow in under an hour. Her mother greeted her at the door, looking as lovely as ever. Ally could see the strain on her mother's face from doing everything. Ally was sure her mother didn't want to worry all of them with how taking care of her dad was affecting her.

"How was your trip, dear?" asked her mother.

"Smooth, Neal sends his love. Where's daddy?"

"He is taking a nap right now. He always goes down after lunch. I had hoped he would be up to greet you, but he will be shortly. Let's get your stuff in your room."

Ally followed her mother to the front door again and then down the front hall. They had a spacious four-bedroom home on a golf course. They use one as a study. The master was on the opposite side of the house, near the family room. It was a roomy home with an open floor plan. The nicest room was the veranda, as they call a patio in Florida. After she took her suitcase into her room and removed a few items she wanted to hang in the closet, she went to the kitchen, where her mom had placed sandwiches and lemonade on a tray. They carried it outside and sat at the round table where they eat most of their meals. Her mother had redecorated her kitchen, using the same colors as those on the veranda. Ally complimented her on the colors. She wished she had her mother's taste in decorating.

Ally wasn't sure if this was the right time to discuss what she had come here for; since she was only there for three nights, she knew she had no time to waste.

"How are Janet and Adam, Mom?"

Her mother sighed, "They are very sad. I haven't spoken with Janet one time on the phone that she didn't burst out crying."

"I would expect that. I haven't called her since we returned, and I feel bad about that. I couldn't bring myself to discuss it."

"I wish you would call her. She leaned on you so much during the funeral. I could see how close you became."

"You're right. I owe her that. I was considering flying there before I go home. I will check with Neal and see if he would mind if I extended my trip."

"That would be good of you. She would love it."

"Mom, I have something I need to discuss with you, and I don't know quite how to do it. Can we talk now?"

"Of course, anything wrong?"

"You can tell me; you see, I sent my DNA in after we returned from Rachel's funeral."

Ally saw her mother's face turn to stone. She had seen that look before, but not since she was a teenager. "Why would you do that, Ally?' she recovered and smiled.

"Why wouldn't I?"

"I don't know. I didn't think you were interested in that kind of thing. No reason, just a little surprised."

"I got my results. Dad is not my father, is he?"

Gloria looked down at her lap, as if she had a note card there that had the answer. "I need a minute."

She rose, went to the family room, and came back with a box of tissues. She gently placed it on the table between them.

"I wanted to tell you so many times, but I didn't have the courage."

"Does dad know?" asked Ally.

"No, no one does."

After a few minutes of silence, her mother looked her in the eye and told her the truth.

CHAPTER 17

"In about 1969, Bill Fitzgerald and his wife, Geri, moved to Eldridge. They were from Boston, and both grew up there. They were ready to move to a small town, take it easier. Bill was a fourth-generation policeman. His father was a Captain, and Bill was enamored of his father. He never thought he would come close to reaching the same level. He said many times that he was a little fish in a great big pond.

"He made it a point to meet with all of Eldridge's business owners and learn their needs. He hired more patrolmen and women once the Town Council freed up funds. The town was growing, and the same problems plaguing big cities were creeping into Eldridge. It wasn't too bad yet, but that was one thing about Bill; he didn't wait. He was proactive, not reactive.

"Geri was a lot of fun. We got along great. She loved playing tennis and was very active in the club. They had an adopted son, Aaron. She told me they tried for years, but she couldn't get pregnant. She felt like a failure. As a good Catholic girl who was not pregnant, she was stressed. They somehow were able to adopt Aaron. He was left at the local fire department. The fireman who found him called Bill immediately. There was no doubt that Bill would adopt him. I often wondered if any shenanigans took place, but that was a conversation no one had.

"Aaron was a year younger than Craig, so they played sports together. He would remember Aaron. I believe he went to college out west and became an engineer. We lost touch with them, but I am getting ahead of myself.

"One day after a tennis match, we were changing to get ready to go out to lunch. She asked me to look at something under her left arm and close to her breast. It was a lump. I asked her how long it had been there. She said it had been about a month, and it had gotten bigger.

"I told her she needed to check into it and referred her to my doctor. The following week, she went in to have it biopsied. Unfortunately, it came back positive. She was scheduled for a mastectomy. I was with her the morning she went in for surgery. She was crying, and so was I.

"After she had healed well enough, she went for chemotherapy and radiation. She had a very rough time of it. Her hair fell out, and she wore a scarf until she found a wig she could manage. She hated wearing a wig.

"Once the treatment started, she was so ill. I stayed with her until Janet and Craig came home from school in the afternoon. Aaron spent a lot of time at our house.

"Geri was very brave, but the treatment took such a toll on her. She lived eight months after her last treatment. Bill called me on Christmas Eve and told me she had passed. That was 1970.

"I was inconsolable. Your father did his best, but he was trying to keep his business going while also helping at home. He was so good like that. Bill also had his moments. His mother stayed with him and Aaron for about three months. Geri was a great woman and a wonderful friend. I loved her like the sister I never had. Her death left a void in my life.

"What I'm about to tell you now will be shocking, Ally. I wanted to provide you with some background so you can put everything in context and understand what happened next.

I was at home, working on correspondence with my family, when there was a knock at the door.

"Bella, our Cocker Spaniel, started barking, so I got up to see who was there. I could see through the peephole that it was Bill. Of course, I wasn't expecting him. Your father had already left for work, and I wondered if they had an appointment he had forgotten. I opened the door, and Bill said, "May I come in?" I panicked, thinking something had happened to John.

"Of course, I let him in and asked if something had happened to John.

"He assured me, John was fine and said he only wanted to come by and thank me for everything I did for Geri. He gave me a bracelet he had given to her. It was a tennis bracelet. He told me she loved it so much and that he wanted me to have it to wear in her memory.

"I remembered her wearing it every day, and she had told me that when they moved to Eldridge, Bill gave it to her for an anniversary gift. I was very moved.

"I took it from him very gingerly, and he helped me put it on my left wrist. I broke down and started sobbing. He put his arms around me and consoled me. That was when our affair began. Neither of us meant it to happen, I swear. We weren't those people. We were so brokenhearted that the only way we could get past our grief was to be together.

He kissed me that day, and I kissed him back. He backed away, told me it was wrong, and apologized. I did the same; however, we kissed again. That time it was more passionate. He was there for about an hour. We didn't make love that day, although I believe he wanted to, and I did as well. Believe me when I say, Ally, this was not because of anything John had done or not done. I had a great husband and a great life. It just happened."

"How long?"

"How long what?" she asked.

"How long did the affair last?" asked Ally, trying not to be stern, but she thought her mother took it that way.

"I don't like that word, 'affair'," said Gloria.

79

"Isn't that what you call it when a married woman sleeps with another man, whether he is married, widowed, or divorced?" asked Ally.

Stunned by her daughter's words, Gloria said, "Yes, you're right. I'm being defensive, and you don't deserve that. It lasted two months. We slept together four times. I was on birth control, and he used a condom, because of the times, STDs, and all, but I became pregnant."

"How were you sure it was his and not Dad's?"

"I figured it out the old-fashioned way. Your father went to a conference in Boston a week after we started sleeping together, and I was with him twice during that week. Your father was gone for a week, from Sunday until Friday. We didn't see each other for at least two more weeks because Bill was out of town. He took Aaron on Spring Break to his mother's, who lived in St. Petersburg. We saw each other again and then broke off. It was hard because we loved her so much, and with us out of each other's lives, a little part of Geri died all over again. Do you understand?"

"How did you tell Dad?"

"I went to the doctor and confirmed it after I missed two periods, and when he came home that night, I told him."

"Was he happy?" asked Ally.

"Elated," he always wanted another child. He adored you."

"And I adore him," Ally started crying and put her head on her mother's shoulder. Gloria comforted her youngest child the best she could.

"Does dad know I'm not his?" asked Ally.

They both heard the sound at the same time and quickly ran to the room where Ally's dad was sleeping. He was on the floor.

Ally kneeled at his head to assess the situation. "He is awake. Call 911. She felt all around his head and neck for bleeding, and finding none, she gently rolled him from his side to his back, being careful to hold his head in a neutral position.

Gloria ran into the room holding the phone and saying, "My daughter is here, and she is a nurse, he is on his back and appears to be awake."

Ally motioned for her mom to give her the phone, and her mom did. "Hello, this is Ally Smith. I'm his daughter and also a retired nurse. I am here at his side. Please send the ambulance, I think he needs to be checked out in case he fractured something. Okay, that's fine."

"They are on the way." She looked at her mom and could see how pale she was. "Sit down, Mom. He is fine, they'll be here soon."

CHAPTER
18

After they arrived at the hospital, her father was taken to radiology for an X-ray. The E.R. doctor suspected a broken hip, but there could be more injuries, they were told.

Ally told her mother she was going outside to call Janet and Neal, but that she would be right back. Her mother sat solemnly and softly said, "He never knew."

"Knew what?"

"That you may not be his. I always thought you were his, I really did. Please believe me."

"I do believe you, Mom. I'll be right back."

"Okay, thank you."

Ally had tears in her eyes as she pulled up and hit call on Neal's number.

Neal answered right away, and when she told him about her father, he said he would make arrangements to fly down immediately.

"It's okay, you don't have to come right away. He may be fine; we're waiting on X-rays. He was conscious and didn't appear to have hit his head on anything. He was nonverbal and didn't know what was happening to him. He looked scared, Neal," her voice cracked, and he knew she was about to cry.

"I'm so sorry, darling. I'll let Mary know. I'm sure she will be happy to take Lucky for a few days, if needed. Please call me as soon as you have the test results. I'll be happy to talk with a surgeon if he needs surgery."

"Okay," she said, wiping away tears. "I had a long talk with my mother about the other situation."

"How did that go?"

"As well as could be expected. I'll call you later when I have more privacy and tell you all about it."

"Okay. I love you."

She hung up and called her sister, Janet. She got her voicemail recording. "Hi, Janet. It's me. Please call me as soon as you receive this message. It's about Dad."

She returned to the waiting room in the radiology area. The hospital was cold. She asked the tech if she and her mom could have a couple of warm blankets, and the tech got them each one.

"Do you want me to get you a cup of coffee, Mom?"

"No, not right now. My stomach is too upset right now. Let's wait to get the results."

"That's fine." Ally wished she had brought a book. She had her phone but didn't like reading on it. She thought she might need glasses. She had forgotten to make the appointment with the doctor Neal suggested.

****

They were getting restless when a very young man, apparently of Indian descent, rounded a corner and entered the waiting room. "Mrs. Malcom?"

"Yes," Gloria stood when he said her name.

Ally stood up with her, gently cuffing her mother's elbow.

"I am Dr. Patel, and I reviewed your husband's X-rays. It appears he has a dislocated right hip. He will need a reduction to get the head back in the socket."

"So, there are no breaks or fractures?" Ally asked him.

"None that we could see on an X-ray. After the reduction, he will have a CT scan to confirm everything is stable and to check for any fractures that may have revealed themselves. I'm going to inform the ER doctor of our findings, and they will consult with a surgeon. Any questions?"

"Is he awake?" Gloria asked.

"Yes, he is awake. Come with me, and you can see him."

They followed Dr. Patel down a sterile-looking hallway to a room that was even colder. He was on the stretcher, lying flat with his eyes closed.

"John," whispered Gloria. He opened his eyes and smiled at her.

"Hi, Daddy," said Ally. He looked over at her and also smiled, but she couldn't tell if he recognized her or not. She decided not to press the matter for now.

The tech came to the head of the stretcher and said, "Okay, Mr. Malcom, we are going for another ride."

They returned to the same E. R. room where he was hooked up to the monitor. Ally could see that he was in a normal heart rhythm with a pulse of 72 beats per minute. His pacemaker shouldn't have been affected.

They each took a chair at opposite sides of his stretcher. He said, "Why am I here?"

Gloria told him that she and Ally found him on the floor of their bedroom.

"Who is Ally?"

Ally turned white as a ghost and looked at her mother. Gloria gave her a sign with her eyes, letting it pass for now. She thought perhaps he had been under stress and, not realizing she was coming, he may have had a momentary lapse of memory.

"Ally came down from North Carolina to see us. Wasn't that nice?"

"Yes, that was nice." He looked over at his youngest daughter and smiled again. This time, he seemed to recognize her. His eyes became brighter. Ally, who was holding her breath, sighed. *Maybe he is not as far gone as I thought.*

They waited for what seemed an eternity, but was only forty minutes, when a doctor came in. "Hello, I am Dr. Chastity Hope."

Ally almost laughed, but caught herself and held out a hand to her. She shook it, turned to Gloria, whom she knew must be the wife, and held out her hand. Gloria took it and told her, John was her husband.

"What can you tell us?" asked Gloria.

"He does need a reduction of the right hip. It is a simple procedure; however, I do recommend a light sedation, such as propofol, for his comfort. It can be quite uncomfortable, especially for an older adult. He looks rather fragile."

Her mother turned to Dr. Hope so that John couldn't see her face and mouthed, "He has Alzheimer's."

Dr. Hope acknowledged what she said with a nod. Ally knew she would have seen it in his chart if she had read it. She went to his bedside and picked up his left hand. He looked at her with a blank stare. "I am Dr. Hope, Mr. Malcom. You need to have your hip fixed, and I would like to take care of it today. You may experience some discomfort, and if it isn't addressed, there could be damage to your blood vessels and nerves in that leg. Is it okay with you to do that?"

He nodded and looked at his wife. She nodded at him and smiled. "You'll be fine, John. Just a little hiccup and then you'll be able to go home, and we can enjoy our visit with Ally."

"Yes, we can," he said, without looking at Ally. *A bad sign?*

"Dr. Hope, my husband is a recently retired anesthesiologist, and he would like to speak with you before the procedure. Would that be okay?"

"Sure, is he here now?"

"No, he is in North Carolina, but I can call and get him on the phone really quickly."

"Yes, please. I'll wait."

Ally called Neal's cell phone and told him she had the surgeon who was willing to talk with him. She handed the phone to Dr. Hope, and she stepped outside the curtain to speak with him.

After just about a minute, she came back into the room and handed the phone to Ally.

"Neal?"

"Yes, everything is set. What she planned for the reduction sounds fine. Normally, an E.R. physician could do it; however, with his mental condition, they felt taking him to the OR would be safer. She is aware of his Alzheimer's. He will be fine."

****

The nurse came in and had her mother sign the consent for surgery. Ally assured her it was necessary; though she knew it could be done without anesthesia, it was better with it. Her father had lost so much weight, and she thought he would be in too much pain.

It was another hour before the surgical nurses came to get him. They followed protocols. Ally was impressed with this hospital so far. In the meantime, Janet had called her, and they spoke through the speaker so her mother could hear as well. She asked them to call her as soon as it was over, and Ally assured her they would.

After her father left the room, Ally looked at her mother and said, "Let's pray."

CHAPTER

19

Her father was in recovery, and they were waiting for an observation room. Dr. Hope had already spoken with them, and she said everything went as expected. He is to have a CT scan shortly, and then he will be in a room for an overnight stay.

Her mother said she was getting hungry, so they went to the cafeteria. "We'll call Janet while we're eating," said Ally.

They got their meal and found a table. Ally called Janet.

"Hi, Janet. I have you on speaker. Mom and I are having an early dinner."

"Hello, Mother. Are you okay?" asked Janet, always concerned about her parents, both of them.

"I'm fine, dear. How are you?"

"Hanging in there. Adam went back to work last week, and it was lonely for a few days, but I'm getting some things done. I helped Evan's mom clean out their apartment. That was hard, and I'd rather not talk about it now. How's Dad?"

Ally said, "He is fine, according to the doctor. He will spend the night, out of precaution, I think, due to his Alzheimer's."

"That's good. You and Mom can have some mother-daughter time."

Ally looked at her mother, and she could see the same strain on her face that she was feeling in that moment. They were never very close, and the secret they shared had driven a wedge between them. Of course, Janet knew nothing about that. This wasn't the time to go into it; in fact, she wasn't sure she ever would.

"We will, I'm sure. A lot to talk about. Right, Mom?"

"Yes, I want to hear all about your honeymoon. Well, maybe not everything," she chuckled.

Ally laughed along with Janet. There are some things moms and daughters get without saying a word.

They finished their dinner and headed back to the observation suite. The desk nurse gave them his room number. He didn't hear them when they entered. After Gloria shook him by the shoulder, he started and opened his eyes.

"What happened?" he asked her.

"Ally and I found you on the floor at home, and you were brought to this nice hospital, and you had a minor surgery."

"Who is Ally?" he asked.

Ally said, "Daddy, it's me. I came to see you and Mom."

His eyes betrayed his confusion about who she was, but he recovered and said, "I'm glad you came."

"Me too," said Ally.

****

On their way home, they stopped at CVS, and her mother picked up some headache medication. Ally needed to pick up toothpaste because she forgot to pack hers. It was around nine o'clock in the evening, and it was still very warm outside.

"I don't know how y'all live here year-round. I still enjoy having some cooler weather."

"How was Italy?" her mom asked.

"Oh, it was great. We had a lovely time on the cruise and met so many nice people. There weren't any issues, except I probably spent too much money. I have something for you and Daddy, by the way."

"You're very sensible with your spending, Ally. I always admired that about you."

"You admired me? Really?"

"Yes, darling. You were the most practical of all of my children. Craig had to be reigned in at times about his spending."

Gloria was an only child and had a Trust Fund left to her by her great-grandfather on her mother's side. He made his money in real estate. She never touched the fund until her children were born, and then she started dividing it among them. She was fortunate to stay home with her children, but mainly because she always knew the trust fund was there as a safety net.

"Mom, you never told me that you admired me."

"I didn't?"

"Not that I remember."

"I'm sorry if I didn't. You're not upset with me, are you?"

"No, I'm too old to be upset about anything. It's water under the bridge."

"Ally, do you think I was a good mother?"

"Yes, Mom. I do think you were a good mother, even a great mother. It's just that I always thought you treated me a little differently. I thought it was because of the age difference between Craig and me. I don't know, maybe it was my imagination."

"I did treat you differently, Ally. I admit it. You were special and in a good way. I want you to know that. Do I wish my indiscretion with Bill had never happened? Yes, probably. But then I wouldn't have you, so I cannot say that."

"Did you absolutely know I couldn't have been Dad's?"

"I was fairly certain, yes. I hoped I was wrong, but gestational charts are pretty accurate, and I knew when, you know, we met up."

"When you had sex with Bill?"

"Yes."

The rest of the drive home was quiet. In fact, they said good night as they entered the house, and Ally went to her bedroom. She had all kinds of thoughts going through her mind, and she needed to concentrate.

She called Neal after she got into bed. "Hi, darling," he answered.

"How are you?"

"I'm good. Well, that's not true. My mother and I had a conversation that turned negative as we were driving home from the hospital."

"Anything serious?" asked Neal.

"Just that she tried to tell me I was special in a good way because I had a different father. I don't think she meant it to sound the way it did, but it was an awkward admission, and I got graphic, which she didn't appreciate. You know me. Always putting my foot in my mouth."

"Maybe she needed to hear how you felt, Ally. You can't keep putting frosting on this hot mess."

"You're right, as usual. So wise. That is just one of the reasons I love you so much."

"The other being that I take care of your cat whenever you leave?" he asked.

"Ah, you know, he became your cat when we married. Kind of like adopting a kid I might have had."

Neal laughed. "You got me there. How's your dad?"

"I realized before we left the hospital that he had no idea who I was. I won't go into it, but suffice it to say he had a blank look in his eyes."

"That's too bad. I'm sorry. Is he coming home tomorrow?"

"I don't know yet. We'll find out when we get there. I'll call you when I have more information. I'm half thinking about flying to Houston to see Janet and Adam. Would you mind?"

"No, of course not. Lucky will keep me company."

"I was hoping you wouldn't mind. I feel that I need to see them."

"Are you planning on telling Janet?"

"I don't know yet, what do you think?"

"I would weigh the pros and cons first."

"Again, wise man. I love you. Good night."

"Good night."

After they hung up, Ally sat for a few minutes, then decided to go to her mother to see if she was still up. She didn't want to go to sleep without clearing the air.

She reached her mom's room, but it was dark, and her mother was already asleep. She waited, heard her lightly snoring, and tiptoed back to her room to go to bed. It had been a long day.

CHAPTER
20

"Did you sleep well?" her mother asked as soon as she entered the kitchen.

"It was okay. How about you?"

"I did. Me and my Ambien."

"I take it sometimes, too. Luckily, I've been a good sleeper most of my life. As I get older, it is harder, so I understand people who need something to help."

Her mother handed her a cup of coffee.

"Thanks," said Ally.

She reached for the cream and sugar. "I still need something in mine. It is too bitter."

"I forced myself to drink it black a while back, and I like it better."

"Mom, I am sorry about last night. I was out of line."

"That's okay, I didn't get upset. You were always honest about your feelings, so I'm glad that you said it."

"Good, I hope we can keep an open communication. Also, I asked Neal last night about going to Houston to see Janet and Adam, and he was okay with it. I want you to know, I don't plan to say anything to Janet about what I learned. I feel it isn't my place, not my story to tell. Well, maybe a little, but I don't want her to hear it from me, so if you want to keep it between us and not tell Janet or Craig, it is fine with me."

"Wow, I hadn't thought of that. Thank you, Ally. I will think about it. It was and is my story, and they should hear it from me. I regret not telling your father, but in a way, I'm glad. I'm experiencing a multitude of paradoxical feelings right now. I wonder if I need to see a therapist?"

"It wouldn't hurt. I've been to a therapist before," said Ally.

"Oh, really? About what?"

"Mother, that's the whole reason for therapy, to talk about what you cannot talk about with other people, so I would rather not say."

"I'm sorry, you're right. Please forget I asked, okay?" She put a hand over Ally's.

"You're forgiven," said Ally.

****

They left to pick up Ally's father from the hospital. Her mother insisted on driving because she thought he would be confused if he were in a different car.

"That's a good idea, Mom."

When they arrived at the room, the tech was already there, helping him change his gown. Gloria thought that was strange. "Isn't he going home?" she asked.

"I'm only doing as I was told, so I'm not sure. I'll be right back."

A nurse came in a few minutes later and informed them that the doctor wanted to discuss his discharge. She offered to page him.

"Thank you," said Gloria.

It wasn't too long before a doctor came into the room and introduced himself as Bryce Simpson. "I'm the PA working with your husband. We feel he would do better in an assisted care home for a few days, perhaps a week. He has a cracked rib on his left side. He had quite a fall. We want to ensure he has time to heal and his hip is stable. I'm sure he will do well and be home soon."

"Was that found on the CT scan?" asked Ally.

"Yes, we did find it on the CT, but it was also on his X-ray. The hip was a much greater concern at the time. He will do fine if there isn't another fall."

"Okay, what do we do?" Gloria asked.

"Our care coordinator will be in shortly, and you can decide where you want him to be moved. I'm afraid our places are limited, so you may not get your first choice."

"I understand."

"How are you, John?" asked the PA.

"I'm doing okay."

"Did you eat breakfast?" he asked.

"Yes, I ate everything." Gloria smiled because she knew he probably hadn't eaten everything, but he knew the doctor wanted to know he had, so he played along. She knew the PA would look in the chart and find out.

"Okay, I'll let you continue to rest and visit with your family," then he left the room.

Ally said, "I'm going to step out to call Neal and check in, okay, Mom?"

"Sure, that's fine."

****

"Hi, darling. How are you?" Ally asked when Neal picked up.

"I'm fine. Getting ready to go pick up Roger and go fishing."

"Oh, I forgot. I won't keep you. Dad won't be coming home. He has a cracked rib on the left side, and they think he needs to go to an assisted living facility."

"It's probably best. How's your mom?"

"We had a hard conversation this morning. I'll tell you later, but we are good now. You and Roger have a great time. I'll give Mary a call in a little bit. She's probably at the pool doing aerobics."

"I hope you and your mom have a better day. I'll talk to you later tonight."

"I love you," said Ally.

"Me too, you."

She went back to her dad's room. They were quietly talking, so Ally tiptoed in, but her mother sensed her presence and turned around.

"Did you get Neal?"

"Yes, he and his friend are going fishing this morning. He's excited to get out there."

"That's nice. I hope they catch a lot of fish. Don't you, hon?" she looked at John.

He only smiled at her.

It wasn't long after that when a young woman came into the room and said she was there to review the arrangements for moving him to a facility. They discussed the location, and because there are so few beds available, they had to accept the one in Lakeland. This meant it would be a longer drive, but Ally knew her mother would make it a priority to see her father every day.

When they got back home that afternoon, Ally made arrangements to fly to Houston the day after tomorrow. Her brother, Craig, wanted to see her before she left. The situation with their dad had prevented them from making dinner plans. It occurred to her she could stop by and have lunch with him, since her flight was in the mid-afternoon. She was going to call him later. Her mother agreed to wait until tomorrow morning before going to the facility. Her father was to be transferred later that same day.

CHAPTER 21

Ally was in the waiting area for a Delta flight to Houston. Her sister insisted on picking her up at the airport. She was glad because she was exhausted from all the things she had to take care of during her visit to her parents'.

Her father was transferred as planned, and the facility was nice. Ally and her mother went there the morning after he was moved, and spent about five hours with him. Her father had two physical therapy sessions while they were there, and they were able to see him during therapy. He appeared to cooperate with the therapist and didn't seem to be in any pain, although Ally knew many Alzheimer's patients would deny pain when asked. She made a mental note to tell her mother that before she left for Houston.

They decided to go out to eat after they left the facility. Her father had a good lunch, so they felt they could leave him afterward, knowing he had been fed.

"He'll be fine, Mom. I know you are concerned, but they won't discharge him until he is ready. They will continue to come to the home until he is strong enough, and they will ensure there are no obvious hazards. Daddy's in relatively good health, so he should get stronger, with additional physical therapy."

"I'm concerned, you know, for other reasons."

"Alzheimer's?"

"Yes," said Gloria with tears in her eyes.

Ally felt sorry for her mom in that moment. Her life as she knew it was over. She now had a new life, for better or worse. Ally just spoke those words a few months ago, when she and Neal tied the knot. Of all people to get Alzheimer's, she thought her father was too brilliant to be struck with no memory. It truly doesn't discriminate.

They ate slowly, their appetites sapped by stress. Ally thought her mother needed therapy for her mental health, but she wouldn't dare bring it up again. She was looking forward to leaving the next day, after having lunch with her brother, to fly into Houston. She doesn't plan to discuss her discovery with her siblings, at least until her mother has told them or given her permission.

"Mom, I have enjoyed having this time with you and Daddy. I'm glad I could help you. Thank you for being so honest about the discovery I made. Again, it is your place to tell Janet and Craig. You'll know when the time is right. Keep in mind, they may find out on their own someday, as I did."

"Funny you should say that. I have been trying to figure out what I am going to say to both of them," said Gloria.

"You'll have a lot of time to think about it," Ally tried to comfort her.

****

When the plane arrived at its gate, she texted Janet, giving her time to leave the Text Lot and drive to Arrivals. She still had to pick up her luggage. After the bathroom break, she made her way to the assigned luggage carousel and found hers quickly.

Janet was there when she walked out of the terminal. They hugged so tightly that Ally felt crushed. Janet started crying.

"I'm so glad you are here. It's so quiet at our house, like a tomb. I cannot stand it. I know Rachel had moved out of the house, but it wasn't that long ago, and just knowing she won't ever be walking through the door again makes me so sad. I'm a hot mess, Ally."

"Let's get going. These security guards are neither patient nor friendly," said Ally.

Ally didn't expect Janet to be dressed up for a car ride, but she noticed she hadn't even combed her hair or put on makeup. It was almost seven in the evening, and she looked like she had just crawled out of bed.

"Are you hungry?" Janet asked her.

"No, I'm fine. I had a big lunch with Craig. It was good getting to see him for a change. He seemed content with his career choice. I can't help but wonder why he won't propose to his girlfriend."

"Maybe it is her? I mean, some women are not ready to settle down," Janet suggested.

"At her age? Of course, I'm one to talk. I'm pushing fifty-five and just got married. She has to be at least my age, or did he go for a real young one?"

"She isn't really young, but I think there is about a twenty-year age difference. She'd be hitting menopause, I would think."

"Twenty years?"

"Craig is sixty; he will be retiring in a few years. I believe he plans to teach once he retires. He can't possibly keep up with physical therapy for too many more years," said Janet.

"We are all getting older. Remember when we were young and had no cares in the world? We would go to the beach house and have Grandma Harriett spoil us all summer."

"I remember. Those were the days. No responsibility, didn't think anything bad would ever happen to us," Janet started tearing up again.

Ally stopped talking, hoping she would get past it. She has to be careful and not say anything around Janet about losing Rachel. *This is going to be a rough trip,* she thought. She could tell they were approaching their subdivision. The landscape changed once you left the Houston area. They lived southwest of Houston and had been affected by the hurricane season many times.

Janet pulled into the gated community, having the gate open for her because of the car sticker on her front plate. It is very small but powerful. Ally remembered Adam telling her and Neal about it when they were in Charlotte, back when things were better.

"Oh, good, I see Adam is here. I hope he picked something up to eat. I'm starved."

"We could've stopped to eat. I'm sorry," Ally apologized.

"No, that's okay. I knew I was too much of a mess and shouldn't go into a restaurant. I was cleaning all day and never got a shower."

That explains the way she looks, thought Ally.

She gave Adam a big hug. He brought her bags into the house and placed them in the guest room. They had a very large home. It was the one the kids grew up in. Ally had thought they would've sold and moved to something smaller. It's probably best they never did, but now they had so many memories to process.

"How was your trip?" asked Adam.

"Great, the plane trip at least," she laughed.

"So, John is okay?"

"As well as can be expected. He's in good hands. Mother was worried about bringing him home, but I assured her that a nurse would be assigned for home PT for a while. I think she should hire someone to help with him, after that."

"I've been trying to get her to do that for a long time," said Janet as she rummaged in the freezer for something to fix for dinner, since Adam hadn't picked up anything. "Ah, found it. I thought I had put a lasagna in here the last time I made it. I will thaw it out and make a salad to go with it for dinner."

"Sounds good," said Ally.

Over lasagna and a good bottle of red, they talked about many things, especially how well Justin and Ellen were doing. They never once mentioned the wreck. Ally thought that was strange, but then again, they may be trying to get past it. She wondered if they were in grief counselling. She hoped they were.

CHAPTER
22

The following morning, Ally awoke to the smell of bacon. She had to reorient herself to her surroundings. She slept sc deeply, with so many dreams. She and Neal talked on the phone until almost eleven, his time. He told her all about his fishing trip with Roger, including how many fish they caught and released. He said he had a wonderful time and hoped they would make it a regular thing.

She walked into the kitchen and found Janet humming a tune and in a very good mood. She wondered if she and Adam had sex last night. She was already dressed and had make-up on. Ally was pleased to see she wasn't in a depression, as she feared.

"Coffee?" asked Janet.

"I can get it, thank you."

"I'm making pancakes, so bear with me. I broke down and bought a package mix. It's been a while since I made them from scratch."

"No worries," Ally assured her.

"Has Adam left for work?"

"Yes, he's an early bird. They have a gym in the building where he works, so he goes in early to get his workout in before work. It's actually a nice place, and it costs him nothing."

"That's great. I belong to a gym at the local college and take water aerobics. I try to go three days a week, but lately it has been hard."

I shouldn't have said that, thought Ally. *She will think it is due to Rachel's death.*

"I know, it's always something. Right?"

"Right," said Ally, taking a sigh of relief.

Janet was placing the pancakes on a plate kept warm in the oven. She added two slices of bacon. She took the syrup out of the microwave, then put their plates up on the bar.

"I hope you don't mind eating right here."

"Not at all, no need to mess up the table," said Ally.

Ally started eating her pancakes and realized how hungry she was. "Ummm, these are good, Janet."

"I can still cook, just don't always feel like it."

"Well, you hit my weak spot this morning."

"I have news that I forgot to mention to you. Adam and I sent out our DNA to Ancestry. He called a little bit ago and said the results will be delivered today. He was tracking it on the computer. I can't wait to see where we are from and who we are related to. I have friends who have done it, and you wouldn't believe the results they have found, some not so good."

Ally was stunned. Her face went ashen, and she began to shake.

"Are you okay?" asked Janet.

"I think so. Could you get me a glass of water?"

"Yeah, sure."

Ally was sure the same DNA was loaded into Ancestry or 23andMe, even though she had sent hers through a different company. She can't be sure that Bill Fitzgerald didn't send his to both places. She didn't want to take a chance, either.

Once Ally had taken a sip, she said, "We need to talk."

Ally got off the stool, walked over to the kitchen table, and sat down. Janet followed her over there.

"Sit down, Janet. I have something to tell you."

Janet sat down. Ally looked at her and said, "Mother was going to tell you this, but I feel that I must go ahead. I'm not sure how to tell you this, but we are half-sisters."

Janet started laughing, "What are you talking about. Are you trying to pull something over on me? It's not April Fool's, is it?"

"No, not April Fool's. I sent my DNA to a company called GEN-match. It is a company that law enforcement uses to analyze DNA in criminal cases. I got it back just a week or so before I went to Florida. I have a different father. I've had it double-checked; I've sent my saliva for retesting. It's true."

Janet's mouth dropped, and she was eyeing Ally suspiciously. "Do you mean our mother had an affair?"

"That's exactly what I am telling you."

"Did you ask her?"

"Yes, and she told me the entire story. Do you remember their friends, Bill and Geri Fitzgerald? Mom said Geri was her best friend."

"Vaguely, it seems there was a woman she played a lot of tennis with at one time, but didn't she die?"

"Yes, she told me she had breast cancer and passed away, and it devastated Mom."

"Okay, but how did that result in an affair?"

"Loneliness, sadness, grief. Bill initiated it, she said. It lasted just a couple of months, but long enough for her to become pregnant with me. It happened during a business trip Dad took, she thinks."

"How did she know it was definitely Bill's?"

"The 'it' is me," she reminded her. "She told me she was able to figure it out per the gestation period. Dad was thrilled when she told him, and he never was the wiser. She said she thought about telling him many times, but he was so crazy about me, she never had the heart to do so."

"Does he know now?"

"We wouldn't be sure if he would understand if we did tell him. Besides, what difference would it make now? Dad is pretty far gone as far as Alzheimer's goes. I'm sorry to have to tell you that. You have had more than your share of sadness this year. I admire your strength. I wasn't going to tell you or Craig yet, and Mom knew that. We discussed that it was her place. She was trying to figure out a way to tell you and Craig. Please forgive her, Janet. It has been hard on her with Dad's downhill journey."

"I forgive her, of course. I am just so shocked. We would have never known had it not been for Rachel's accident, would we?"

"Probably not. I don't believe Mom would've ever told me."

"Ever?" asked Janet.

"Not sure. Probably not."

"I know I told you I had heard some wild stories from friends, but this one takes the cake. Of course, I won't be telling anyone about it."

"I hope you mean that. I guess since you know, and Adam, when he gets home, will know, so we probably should call Craig."

"Yes, we should. And let mom know that we know?" asked Janet.

"I'll do that. I was the one who had to tell it, so I should be the one to tell her how it happened. I knew one day it would have to come out, unless," said Ally.

"Unless what?" asked Janet.

"Unless she had passed before we knew, and then we would always have doubts. She wouldn't have affirmed or denied. I would always wonder if something was wrong with the test. I don't know, that's crazy because we do know, and her secret is out."

"Yeah, it is," said Janet, deep in thought.

****

Ally had packed for her flight home the next day. She was looking forward to seeing her husband. She almost felt giddy, but then thought, *You are nearly fifty-five years old, stop it!* She knew she wouldn't.

She and Janet had decided to wait until they told Adam tonight, then Ally would call their mother before calling Craig. Better part of valor told them they needed to inform her that they knew about the affair.

She heard the mudroom door open and close, so she knew Adam had just come home. She was going to wait until Janet called her to come in before joining them. She felt they needed their privacy after a long day.

After just a few minutes, Janet called her to join them on the back porch. Janet had opened a bottle of wine. Adam had removed his suit and was wearing comfortable shorts and an Astros tee shirt. Janet had dressed in a long Astros jersey, which was probably a pajama top. She wore leggings underneath.

Ally poured herself a glass of the wine and settled in the rocker facing Janet and Adam, who were on the wicker settee.

"Is there something I don't know?" asked Adam.

"Why do you ask?" Janet smiled at him.

"The Malcom sisters look a little conspiratorial, that's all. This wine is excellent, by the way."

"Thank you," said Janet.

Ally noted that Janet had looked over at her and nodded. "Adam, we have something to tell you before you open the results of Janet's DNA."

"Okay, what am I missing? Were you adopted?" he looked over at Janet.

"Nothing like that," said Ally. "My father is not Janet's and Craig's father. In other words, the father I always thought was mine isn't mine."

"How do you know?"

"I did my DNA when I returned to North Carolina following the funeral. The results came back, and I was, of course, shocked. I redid the test, and the results were the same."

"Who is your father?"

"A man named Bill Fitzpatrick. He was Chief of Police."

"I remember him. He came to our school, remember Janet?"

"I suppose, but I don't specifically remember him."

"Have you asked your mother about this?"

"I have, and she admitted everything and explained how it happened."

"How?" asked Adam. "No, I think we all know how. What about the why?"

"She and Bill's wife, Geri, were best friends. They played tennis all the time. Geri came down with breast cancer and died. Bill was lonely, and Mom was grieving, too. It happened when he came by the house one day when she was there alone."

"Of course, he would know she was alone," said Adam.

"I didn't think about that, but yes, you're right. He probably planned it. She told me they had slept together only four times, and two of those were when Dad went to Boston for a five-day conference. That was probably when he impregnated her. They took precautions, but it still happened. She never told our dad, Janet."

"Wow. Is he still living?"

"I'm not sure. I haven't gotten that far. I'm still in shock."

"Are you going to look for him?" asked Janet.

"What do you think?" Ally retorted.

CHAPTER 23

Ally was seated on the plane and anxious to be home. It had been a tiring trip for many reasons. She was ready to get back to work and her routine. She hoped Adam and Janet would be okay. They are still deeply in love after all these years. They knew each other in grammar school, were always together; there was no doubt they would marry one day. They now have only Justin, but Janet believes that Justin and Ellen will have children, so that she will leave grandchildren as her legacy. Ally felt Janet would always wonder what Rachel's children would have looked like; that's what was so sad about losing a child when they're so young—all of the 'what ifs' that linger.

She called their mom last night and told her Janet and Adam now knew her secret. When she explained why she had to tell them, her mother said she understood. They decided to wait and tell Craig later. They would rather be with him when he found out. Her mother agreed that it would be best. She said that the plan was for her father to come home in a couple of days. They had sent a nurse to the house to ensure everything was set up and that he would be safe. Thankfully, they already had a walk-in shower with a seat where he could be bathed.

She had so much on her mind. She wanted to find her birth father, but felt odd about doing it while the only father she knew was still living. Then again, he was declining fast. She didn't think he knew his children anymore, and it was just a matter of time before he wouldn't know her mother either. It made Ally so sad to think of what was coming.

Neal was there to pick her up when she arrived. She was so happy to see him. "I love you, darling," she whispered in his ear while he was hugging her.

"I love you, too."

On the drive from the Myrtle Beach airport to their home, Neal peppered her with questions about her dad, Janet, and Adam. She filled him in on how Janet reacted when she learned she was her half-sister. "She was shocked, just like I was. Adam was more subdued; he seemed to find it surreal. I mean, how many people does this happen to?"

"I don't know, but I'd bet it is more than you would think. Only those who are interested in their ancestry would discover it, unless another family member had already found it. There are probably some statistics on those who have done their DNA and found a close relative they didn't know about."

'I'm sure you're right. How's Lucky?"

"He's just fine. Fed, petted, and brushed. He is happy," Neal teased her.

"I'll call Mary when I get home and fill her in. I called Diedre from the airport and told her what was going on. She was surprised but not shocked. She said her neighbor found a whole family of relatives during her search. Apparently, the father, who had passed, had another family. Wild, huh?"

"I'd say. Was the mother of her neighbor still living?"

"I forgot to ask, but she didn't mention her."

****

"Hi, Lucky. I missed you," Ally picked up her cat and loved on him. Lucky was a foundling when she first moved to North Carolina. He showed up on her doorstep two days after she moved in. She had never had a pet while living in New York City. She had to think hard about keeping him, but she was so in love with him after a few short hours that his fate was sealed. He was hers. She named him appropriately.

Neal brought in her heaviest suitcase and took it to the master. "What did you put in here? Bricks?"

"No, you're getting out of shape. How about going to the gym with Mary and me? That reminds me, I need to call her."

She found her cell phone in her purse and punched Mary's number.

"Hi, Mary. It's me, I'm back."

"Good, are you tired?"

Ally looked at the clock and saw that it was seven-thirty. North Carolina was an hour ahead of Texas. "A little, could we get together tomorrow?"

"Yes, how about going to the gym and then lunch?" asked Mary.

"That would be fine, but not too early. Pick me up at nine?"

"Sounds good, see you in the morning."

****

Mary had been her best friend since moving to North Carolina. She met her in the first week. She could still see Mary getting out of her car with a casserole in hand and walking up to her in the driveway to welcome her. They hit it off that first evening over a bottle of wine and a plate of lasagna. It didn't take long for them to spend a lot of time together.

Within a few days, in fact, they were already into a mystery from her past. Ally had a college classmate who went missing in 1991. Her skeletal remains washed up on the beach closest to her. She discovered that her parents lived close by and became friends with them. They all eventually became involved in the mystery surrounding the disappearance of Katie Morgan. The case was not definitively solved, but they got close enough that Katie's parents were satisfied with how she probably went missing. Katie had been a kind and resourceful girl who cared deeply for people. Nursing was her calling. It was too bad that she was taken so soon.

Mary also had a mystery in her past that she and Ally became involved in solving. Mary's deceased husband, Tom Hughes, was born after his mother's sister, Mary Hartwell Littlejohn, went missing in Atlanta. She disappeared from a shopping mall in Atlanta. She was never found. Through DNA and a lot of luck, they made contact with Mary's son, Michael. It was quite an experience, as they collaborated with a reporter and a private investigator to uncover the truth. It was quite a discovery, and the families have made contact and kept in touch ever since. They discovered that Mary had staged her own disappearance. It was unfortunate that neither Mary's parents nor her sister, Gladys, who was Tom's mother, lived long enough to know she was safe. Her husband, Michael Littlejohn, had been under suspicion for many years and had to move out of state and even remarried to get from under the media's scrutiny. No one knows what happened to him. Her only child was named after him. She was pregnant when she disappeared.

Ally and Mary had dubbed themselves the 'accidental sleuths'. She liked the moniker. She may even use it sometime in the future, such as a book. But that is just dreaming; she doesn't have time to think about it now.

She proceeded to the master bedroom, where Michael had already showered and was lying in bed reading.

"Good book?" she asked.

"Daniel Silva, you know I like his books."

"Yeah, I remember. I think he might have a new one out. I think I saw it on the shelf in the Hudson shop in the airport in Houston."

"I'll have to look. Coming to bed?"

"After a shower," she winked at him.

CHAPTER 24

After a steamy night with Neal, Ally awoke to the sound of her phone ringing. "Oh, I forgot I'm going to the gym with Mary."

She jumped out of bed. Neal rolled over and grabbed her arm just as she was about to stand. "It's okay, it is only seven, and that was my alarm. I changed the sound on it. I'm sorry."

She turned and punched him in his right upper arm. Then she proceeded to the bathroom. Afterward, she was too awake to sleep again, and the light was coming in through the shade. She went to the kitchen and put a pod in the Keurig. She realized she had not eaten last night after arriving home. Neal had a chicken casserole in the refrigerator that Mary had brought over. She took such good care of him when she had to be away. He told her it was delicious, but she just wasn't hungry. She knew she had lost a few pounds from the stress of her father's hospitalization and the revelation she presented to Janet after she told her they had sent in their DNA. It seems as though the more that is thrown at her, the more that keeps coming.

Enough pity party, she thought. She picked up her cup of coffee and sat on the sofa. The newspaper was on the coffee table, and she picked it up to find out what she had missed since she left. She also turned on the news. The paper ran a major story about a nearby community that had elected a school board member she supported. The county proposed building another high school due to overcrowding. The county was growing faster than it could hire teachers and was short on classroom space. Trailers had been brought in to help with the upcoming school year, which seemed like a solid plan, but the school board member she helped elect opposed it. He came from another state where they had done the same thing when their county was overcrowded, and it had led to funds being misappropriated and a lengthy process to build the new schools. He proposes to go to split sessions. *Even better*, thought Ally. She knew he had a good head on his shoulders. She smiled, knowing she had just a little piece of that victory.

Neal came up behind her and gave her a peck on the cheek. "Thanks for last night."

"You're welcome," said Ally, smiling.

"Do you want breakfast?" asked Neal.

"I do, but I don't want to eat before I work out. On second thought, I'll eat one of my yogurts."

"I'll bring it to you, which one?"

"Black cherry."

Neal brought it over with a spoon and a napkin. "Enjoy."

When she was done, she went to the bathroom, brushed her teeth, then put on her sports bra, shorts, and a T-shirt.

"I'll watch you eat while I wait on Mary."

Neal fixed his regular oatmeal and a banana.

"Want to come with us?"

"Not today, I need to work up to it. Besides, y'all have a lot to discuss."

"That's true. I want to find my father or at least find out what happened to him. I'm hoping Mary will indulge me."

"Did you really think she'd say no?"

Ally laughed. "No, she loves a mystery almost as much as I do."

****

Ally was sitting on the front porch when she saw Mary pull up. She waved and ran down the steps to greet her. She got into the passenger seat, and Mary backed out of the driveway. The beach traffic was heavy this morning, so it took them a while to get on the bypass.

"How are you today?" asked Ally.

"I'm great, how are you?"

"Ready for a workout. I'm not planning on the pool today; were you going to get in?"

"No, I'll wait and go to the next class. So what happened in Texas?"

"Janet informed me they had sent their DNA in, and it came back. Adam was bringing it home. I almost choked on whatever I was eating and had to steady myself. Then I told her."

"What did she say?" asked Mary.

"She was shocked, hurt, probably. I'm not sure. She had all the usual questions, like how I figured it out and who he was. I explained everything my mother had told me. When Adam got home, I had to review everything again. We are all still stunned. It's like you have stepped through the proverbial 'Looking Glass'."

"Oh my. I cannot imagine. It could happen to anyone, Ally. We don't know what our parents did before or after we were born. The same goes for our grandparents, and so on."

"You're right. We all have things in our past we regret. I know I do."

Mary turned and looked at her.

"What? Did you never do anything you have regretted?" asked Ally.

"I'm not sure. I don't like to think so, but I'm sure I have."

They just pulled into the college parking lot and drove to the Aquatic Center. They gathered their things and walked in.

Ally went to the elliptical and worked out for half an hour before doing some weightlifting. Meanwhile, Mary walked on the treadmill for the entire hour.

"I am ready to get out of here and get an early lunch," said Mary. They went to the locker room and tidied up, changing into more suitable clothes for lunch. By the time they arrived at their favorite lunch spot, it had started raining.

"This is wonderful," said Mary. "It hasn't rained in about a month. Everything needs a good drink."

While they waited for their number to be called for food pickup, Ally asked, "Are you up to helping me find my father?"

"I thought you'd never ask."

CHAPTER 25

"What do you know about him?"

"Not a lot, except that he was the Chief of Police in Eldridge. Adam remembered him coming to their school."

"Do you have a picture?"

"There is a Facebook page with a picture, but I'm not sure how current it is. I know he has an adopted son named Aaron. His wife, the one who was my mother's best friend, was named Geri."

"Wait, your mother's best friend was his wife? Really?"

"Yes, but she had passed away from breast cancer, and that is how they got together, according to my mother. She said he came over to the house one day when she was alone. He would have known she was alone, Adam pointed that out to me. Anyway, they grieved together and then fell into each other's arms."

"Allegedly."

"What are you saying, Mary?" Ally asked, irritation in her voice.

"I am just saying you only have one side of the story. There is the other side, and then there is the truth."

"So you think my mother lied to me?"

"I'm not saying she did, or she didn't, but I am only pointing out that we need to find him and get his side."

"Agreed." Ally was upset by Mary's accusation, but she had to admit she was right.

"Hughes and Smith," a voice called out.

"I'll go." Mary got up and picked up their lunch. After sitting back down, she put her hand on Mary's and squeezed it. "It's going to be fine, you'll see."

"What if I hire a private investigator?" asked Ally.

"That's an idea. It may be hard to find out anything without one. I'm just thinking there wouldn't be much on the internet, and whether the Eldridge PD would even give you his records. It's a privacy issue, I would think. What about searching on Facebook for the son?"

"Of course, I could do that."

"Did your mother tell you what year they moved away? That might help in locating the kid in a school."

"Schools are even more tight lipped."

"True, just thinking out loud."

"I don't remember her telling me anything about him after their affair stopped. Huh, I didn't think to ask. I think I was so stunned. I need to call her and see if she can provide me with more information. Now that I think about it, she told me the story the day Dad fell, and after that happened, I never asked her about it again."

"Okay, so you have a plan. Find out from her if she knows when Bill left the area, and we can go from there."

"I also remember her saying my brother and sister played with Aaron, Bill, and Geri's son. I wonder if my brother, Craig, might know something; perhaps he keeps in touch? We haven't told Craig about it yet. Janet and I decided it would be better to tell him in person, and Mom agreed."

"I think you need to contact your brother," said Mary.

"I agree with you, but I'm going to contact my employer first. I haven't spoken with Sarah or Gene since I returned. I'm ready to get back to work. Anything for some normalcy."

They finished their sandwiches and left the restaurant. When Ally got home, she called Three Island Catering and spoke with Sarah.

"I'm back. Anything on the books?"

"Yes, I'm so glad you called. We didn't want to bother you with everything you've had going on."

"I appreciate that, but I'm ready to get back to work. I need something to keep me busy."

"Are you up for a gig tonight? It's a small gathering for a birthday party, but I could give Eliza the night off if you could go."

"I can do it. Would love to, send me the details, thank you, Sarah."

"You've got it." She hung up.

****

Ally looked for Neal when she went through the mudroom. The house was eerily quiet. Lucky was wandering around the house. She walked into the kitchen and saw a note on the counter: *Gone fishing, be back soon.* There was no time on the note, so she has no idea when he will be back. She checked her messages and found a text from Sarah: 5:00, Druid Valley Golf Course, Leland; 60-year-old female; husband is throwing a party.

She checked the time and saw she had only two hours before she had to leave. She checked her closet, found her uniform, and was pleased to discover it was ready to wear. She decided to reach out to Craig to see if he remembered Aaron, but she wanted to speak with Janet first. She called her and left a voicemail, asking her to return the call.

She looked up Aaron Fitzgerald online, but there were too many of them. She found three possible Facebook pages, but there wasn't enough information to track them down. She had noticed that people aren't putting as much personal information on their social media as they used to. *Smart of them*, she thought.

Janet called, and Ally told her she wanted to find her birth father and needed to contact Craig to see if he remembered Aaron. "Mom mentioned to me that you and Craig used to play with Aaron. I hope Craig has kept in touch with him. It's a long shot, but I want to try."

"I get it, go ahead and let me know what you find out. Are you going to let Mom know first?" asked Janet.

"I had not thought about it, but I think not. I don't want his recollections to be skewed. Does that sound sneaky?"

"I don't think so. Trust your gut, Ally."

"Thank you, I'll call you later."

****

Neal got home around three thirty. Ally was putting on her uniform. "Hey, are you working tonight?"

"Yes, relieving Eliza. Sarah asked if I could. Is it okay?"

"Well, I was going to make you some wonderful flounder."

Her eyes got huge, and she said, "Really, you caught some?"

"No, just kidding you. I wish I had. I caught a couple of small speckled trout, but they were too small to keep."

"Not my favorite fish anyway, sorry," said Ally.

"What time will you be home?"

"Not sure, but I would guess about nine. It is in Leland, a birthday party at a golf club. Starts at six. I'll send you the details."

"Okay, I'll just heat something, maybe the steak I fixed while you were gone. It was too much for me, and I froze it."

She kissed him and said, "You won't starve. I've got to run. Try and wait up for me, I have a lot to tell you."

CHAPTER
26

Ally learned from Craig that he and Aaron had kept in touch for a while. He knew that they had moved to Ohio. He wasn't sure, but he thought Springfield.

"Wow, Ally. I'm so sorry. I would have never expected Mom to have an affair. She was always so prim and proper."

"Even the prim and proper have affairs. Maybe because they have more time on their hands and are bored."

"Could be. I'm still stunned. Do you want me to stay quiet?" asked Craig.

"Please, for now. I'll keep you posted on my progress. Janet wants to be kept in the loop, also. I'll let Mom know once I make contact. I would think she would want to know."

"I'm sure she would. Call me anytime. I love you, sis."

"Love you too, Craig."

She brought Neal up to date last night when she got home. He urged her to follow her instincts and find her father if that was what she wanted. He knew curiosity was in her DNA; she was like a dog with a bone until she got the answers.

She called Mary. "Are you busy?"

"No, not really. You want to come over?"

"I do. I'll be there soon."

****

"So, what did you find out?" Mary was anxious to know.

"I spoke with Craig, and he believes they moved to Springfield, Ohio, or somewhere close to there. That's where I'm going to start. Should I check for a listing for Bill? That would be too simple, wouldn't it?"

"You've got to start somewhere."

She pulled out her laptop and looked up the White Pages in Springfield. When she entered William Fitzgerald, about sixty results came up, with various spellings of the name.

"This will take forever. You cannot obtain people's phone numbers anymore without conducting background checks, and that will cost a significant amount. What if I call the police department and ask if they remember him?"

"I don't think they would tell you anything," said Mary.

"I'm going to try, I might get lucky."

She looked up their number online and called. A man answered, "Station Chief Adams, how can I help you?"

"Hello, this is Ally Smith. Could you give me some information about a former employee?"

"First, who are you, and why are you looking for the information? We don't give out personal information on current or past employees."

"Actually, I found out the person I am trying to find is my real father, and I have only the information that he moved from Eldridge, New York, to Springfield, Ohio. His name is William Brian Fitzgerald."

"What year?"

"I believe around 1972 or 1973. Maybe a year or two later. I was born in 1971."

"That is way before my time. I'll have to ask around and see if anyone remembers him."

"He may have been a Chief or another higher ranking. Does that help?"

"It may, yes. What is your telephone number?"

Ally gave him her number. She hoped he was sincere, and nothing would go awry in his research. She was mainly afraid that someone would tell him it wasn't something he should give out. All she can do is pray.

Mary said, "What else can we do now? Did you see anyone else on your DNA report that you didn't know? Perhaps there is a cousin in the mix on his side that would be able to tell you about him."

"I hadn't thought about that. You're a genius."

"Sometimes I get lucky," Mary smiled.

Ally logged into her GEN-match account and found three names she didn't recognize. "Hand me a piece of paper, please."

Ally wrote down the names: Amy Marsh, Stephen Little, and Marsha Michaels.

"Now what do I do. There are no addresses or telephone numbers; how do I reach them?"

"Good question. Perhaps check Facebook and see if any of these lists Eldridge as their hometown?"

"I don't know. He was from Boston, according to Mother," said Ally.

"Start with the male because the women may have married and have a different last name."

Ally pulled up her Facebook account and searched for Stephen Little in Boston. There were too many to count.

"I don't know, it's like a needle in a haystack," said Ally.

"Yes, it is. Not easy to find people without more information. I'm sorry, Ally."

****

When Ally got home, Neal was sitting out on the back deck. She poured a glass of wine and went out to sit with him.

"Any luck?" he asked her.

"No, not really. I called the Springfield, Ohio, police depart-ment and actually spoke with someone. He said he would check whether they ever had a William Fitzgerald. Mary had another good idea. She suggested I check my GEN-match report to see if there were any cousins, so I did, and I found three first cousins whom I didn't know. I tried looking up the only male on Facebook. I looked in Boston, since that was where Bill was from, but there were too many with that name, and many variations. It was like looking for a needle in a haystack. The names are too common, and the women may now be married, which would make it harder. I'm hoping the police department comes through for me."

"That is tough, but don't let it get you down. Want to go out to eat?" asked Neal.

"I would love that, let me finish this wine, and I'll go take a shower and get dressed. Where do you want to go?"

"How about Inlet View?"

"Perfect."

CHAPTER 27

Ally stayed up late the previous evening, searching online for the people whose names had appeared on her DNA report. She knew it was a lesson in futility, but she was determined to find out as much as she could about the man who fathered her.

Neal shared more of his parents' story with her over their meal the night before. She only knew they had passed away, but didn't know the details. He had been an only child and was brought up as a Catholic, attending parochial schools.

He told her, "My mother was a Kennedy. Yes, those Kennedys. However, her father never let anyone know he was related to them. She wasn't aware until her father passed away, and one of Robert Kennedy's children came to the funeral. The cousin had been close to my grandfather when they were young. They got in trouble with the police for stealing a car as teenagers. There was no need to do it. They were doing it on a dare. He got into a lot of trouble, and his mother told him he wasn't to have anything to do with his cousin again, because he was a bad influence. So he never had a relationship with him after that. That was 1962. You know what happened the following year."

"Wow, Neal. Did your mother ever reach out to any of her cousins, albeit it would have been distant cousins by the time they reached her generation?"

"Not that I'm aware. As you know, my parents were killed in a plane crash when I was only nineteen. As far as I knew, there were no Kennedys at their funerals. I was too distraught to pay any attention, though. My father's sister took care of all the arrangements, and I went to live with them afterward."

Ally knew his father was an attorney in Durham, and his mother stayed home. He told her they wanted more children, but it obviously wasn't in the cards; he wished he had siblings to share stories with. "It's barely a memory if you are the only one who remembers it."

She wasn't sure she agreed, but didn't want to disagree with him. Neal was a strong man; he held his parents in high esteem. He wasn't close to his maternal grandparents, but his paternal grandparents and his aunt were loving, and he cared for them. His grandfather died of a heart attack when Neal was in medical school, and his grandmother died of cancer a few years later. He considered his Aunt Phyllis and her husband to be his closest relatives. They had one daughter, Kim, who lived in Michigan. She went to college there and married an engineer. They lived in the suburbs of Detroit. Unfortunately, they never had children.

Ally was going to work a wedding the upcoming weekend. Sarah texted her yesterday, saying they could use her if she were available. She texted her back that she could work and asked her to send the details. From what she received, it would take her about half an hour to get to the venue, a church in Southport. Yesterday, she told Neal she would like to go shopping for clothes. Fall was coming, and she wanted to get a few pairs of slacks and sweaters. Chico's was her favorite place, so she planned to go there today and maybe stop by a discount store like Marshalls. She knew Mary shopped at the one near them and always seemed to find something. Mary had excellent taste in clothes; she wished she could go with her, but she was taking Roger to his doctor appointment this afternoon.

Neal was still asleep, and she didn't want to wake him, so she gingerly got out of bed and went to the kitchen. She first fed Lucky and gave him fresh water. Then she filled the Keurig and made the first cup of coffee of her morning. She unplugged her phone from the charger and saw a voicemail. She checked her voicemail, expecting it to be Mary with a change of plans, but it was the Springfield police department calling. She was asked to return the call to Sargent Barry Newton. She checked the time and saw it was almost eight, so she dialed the number they had left her.

"Sargent Newton," he answered.

"This is Ally Smith returning your call."

"Oh, hello, Mrs. Smith. You called a few days ago inquiring about Bill Fitzgerald?"

"Yes, I did. Did you find anything?" asked Ally.

"We did have an employee by that name in our department. He was a detective when he worked for us. Do you mind me asking what this is about?"

"It is a personal matter, family-related."

"I cannot give out information about current or former employees, but I could contact him and have him call you."

"I suppose that would be okay. Can you tell me if he still lives in the Springfield area?"

"The last information we had, he did not. But I do have a cell number, and with any luck, it is still good."

"You cannot tell me where he moved to, the town? I'm guessing Boston."

"From memory, off the record, I do believe that is where he relocated."

"Thank you for that. Please try to reach him. Say that a friend from Eldridge, New York, is trying to reach him."

"I sure will. If the number isn't good, do you want me to call you back?"

"Yes, I would appreciate a call either way, if you don't mind."

Sargent Newton could hear desperation in her voice. He told her, "Yes, ma'am. I'll let you know."

"Thank you." She hung up.

When Neal got up, she told him about the call.

"I hope for your sake, it's a good number, and you can connect with him, if that is what you want."

"I do want it, but I'm nervous," Ally admitted. "I'm going shopping today. Do you want to come?" she asked him.

"Maybe, where are you going?"

She told him her plans, and he told her he needed some new things, also. They decided to make it an afternoon of shopping.

****

They spent time in Myrtle Beach shopping and eating lunch out. By the time they arrived home, they were exhausted and needed to take naps. The sunroom was so comfortable, and they crashed for a couple of hours. Lucky lay on the ottoman where Neal was resting. Ally took the large settee and had most of the pillows around her. The sun was setting by the time they awakened. Ally realized she had a message from Sarah, asking if she could do a last-minute gig that evening. It was already six, and she would have had to be there at five. She called, but the office was closed. She texted Gene, apologizing for not responding. She knew he was busy, so she didn't expect to hear back. She hoped they found someone else to fill in.

She went to their bedroom, where all of the shopping bags lay, and started taking out their items. She had purchased three pairs of black slacks, each in a different style. One was from Chico's, but the others were from Marshall's. Neal found blue jeans and running shorts. He also picked up some underwear and undershirts. They also bought some much-needed wine glasses. She found a plain white blouse while at Marshalls. She needs those when she's catering. It doesn't take long for blouses to wear out, so she likes to keep a few on hand. It made her even more upset that she had missed the message about helping tonight.

She had not put out anything for dinner, so she rummaged through the freezer and found a lasagna she had frozen the last time she made it. She put it in the microwave to thaw.

Neal came up behind her and kissed her on the neck. "What are you doing?"

"Thawing out a lasagna for us to eat."

"Sounds good." He opened the refrigerator and took out lettuce, cucumber, and a red pepper to make a salad.

"Want some wine?" asked Ally.

"No, not now. I still feel groggy from the nap I took. How about you?"

"I feel that way too. I'm not sure what came over me. Did we walk through a poppy field?" she laughed.

"Makes me wonder," said Neal.

They ate the lasagna while watching the news on TV. "Another shooting, I don't understand it," said Ally.

"It's not going to stop. So many people who want to take out their rage on others. It goes back to mental health, in my opinion."

Ally turned the TV off. "Let's just enjoy our meal without the chatter box."

After cleaning the kitchen, they walked along the beach and then went to bed. They made love for the first time in a week.

"Thank you, Mrs. Smith."

"You're welcome, Mr. Smith," Ally giggled. Their bodies got into a spoon position and gradually fell asleep.

CHAPTER 28

Ally's phone rang during their breakfast, and she saw that it was a Massachusetts number. She immediately answered, "Hello."

"Is this Ally Smith?"

"It is."

"This is Bill Fitzgerald. I believe you left a message for me to call you regarding a personal matter?"

Ally was visibly shaking, and Neal reached over and took her free hand.

"I did leave that message. Are you at home now?"

"I am, why do you want to know, and who are you?"

"I am your daughter."

****

Bill Fitzgerald turned white as a ghost, and that was saying a lot. He had completely white hair and had always been pale with freckles. His legs started shaking, and his stomach turned sour. *What have I done*, he thought.

"Hello, are you there, Mr. Fitzgerald?" asked Ally.

"I am, you just shocked me. What is this about, may I ask? Do you have proof that I have met you before?"

"You have never met me, at least not that I know of. Does Gloria Malcom ring a bell?"

Bill started coughing and had to take a drink of water before he could continue.

"Yes, the name rings a bell."

"Did you live and work in Eldridge, New York?" asked Ally.

"Yes, I did. Oh, no. Do you mean what I think you mean?"

"I'm afraid so, Mr. Fitzgerald. You fathered me when you had an affair with my mother, while she was married."

"How did you find out?"

"DNA, an ancestry site."

"I was listed there?"

"You were. Did you ever give your DNA? Perhaps it was when you were working?"

"Yes, I did. It was a case in Boston just a few years ago. It was a terrible triple murder case, very messy. All the first responders provided DNA samples for testing. That must have been it."

Ally said, "I used GEN-match, which is a site that helps law enforcement. You said you were a first responder?"

"I was the lead detective, so I wasn't the first on the scene but was there very shortly afterward. It was a family annihilation."

"I'm sorry," said Ally.

"It's okay. I've seen a lot in my time."

"I'm sure."

"What has your mother told you about me?"

"Just enough, but I want to know more.

"Would you like to meet me, Ally?"

"Yes, I would. First, I would like to tell my mother I found you. My father, that is the father who raised me, has Alzheimer's, and she is his primary caregiver."

"That is terrible. I remember John very fondly."

I'll bet you do, thought Ally.

"Are you calling me on a cell phone?"

"Yes, it is my cell number; you can call me anytime on it."

"Where do you live?" asked Ally, wanting to know more so she could do more research.

"Canton, Mass. I'm retired now, but I do some side work in security."

"Okay, thanks for calling, and I'll be back in touch." She hung up.

Neal said, "Can I get you anything?"

"No, I'm fine. It wasn't as bad as I thought it would be. I need to think of how I will approach Mom."

****

Ally worked up the courage to call her mother the following morning. She anticipated a difficult conversation, but was pleasantly surprised.

"Hi, Mom."

"Hi Ally, how are you, darling?"

"We're fine, how are you and daddy?" Ally asked her.

"I apologize, I can't get used to you being a 'we' rather than an 'I'. We are doing fine. Your father is getting out and walking short distances. He's getting his strength back. I'm thinking of installing one of those walk-in tubs. A lot of our friends have done it, and they seem to like them. What do you think?"

"I don't know a lot about them. Just make sure you use a reputable contractor to install it. I think it would help you take care of him. You need to take care of yourself."

"I agree. It is quite the ordeal when I have to encourage him into the shower. At least we have a walk-in shower, and I have a shower chair."

"Mom, I'm calling you to let you know something. I found Bill."

Gloria gasped, and she hoped Ally didn't hear her. "That's great, dear. How is he?"

"He seems to be fine. He lives outside Boston and is retired, but he takes on some security jobs. I believe he is in good health if he can still do that."

"That's great. How about Aaron?"

"He didn't mention his son. We had a short conversation. I am going to do more research on him and get back in touch. I just wanted you to know," she told her mother.

"Okay, I understand. Will you meet him if he offers?"

"Actually, he has already offered, if I want to. I honestly don't know. Have you spoken with Janet lately?"

"Yes, just yesterday. She seems to be staying busy. She did tell me that she and Adam are going to Grief Counseling at their church, so that is a good thing, right?"

"I believe it is. I think people need to take care of their mental health because it affects their bodies. I don't want to see their health decline."

Ally knew many marriages fail after the loss of a child, but she hoped and believed Janet and Adam were different. They are faithful and strong people. All she can do is pray for them.

"When do you think you and Neal could come visit?"

"I don't know right now. Let me get back to you on that, okay?"

"That will be fine. You take care."

"You too, Mom. I love you."

"I love you, too."

****

Bill had to take some time to think about how to tell Aaron he had a half- sister. It would dredge up his mother's death all over again. They told him he was adopted when he started middle school. He was curious at the time, but there wasn't anything they could say to him about his mother. They tried to gloss over the part about him being left at a Fire Station. He never brought it up again.

He had just started dating a woman named Marjorie Allen. He met her when he had done a security job at a building near Faneuil Hall in Boston. It was a financial services building. The regular guard had to have surgery, so he filled in for him for about six weeks. The money was good, and the hours weren't bad.

She worked on the ground floor of a securities firm. He had never been good at knowing all of the banking lingo, so she explained what she did over a cup of coffee at Starbucks. They enjoyed talking and found they had a lot in common. She was a widow with twin daughters grown. He learned they lived out of town, and she missed them terribly. He could tell she seemed lonely. They would meet every morning and have coffee, and after two weeks, he could tell there was a spark. He asked her out to dinner, and they have been seeing each other ever since. That was about six weeks ago. He decided to hold on to what he had just learned from her and Aaron about having a daughter until the time was right.

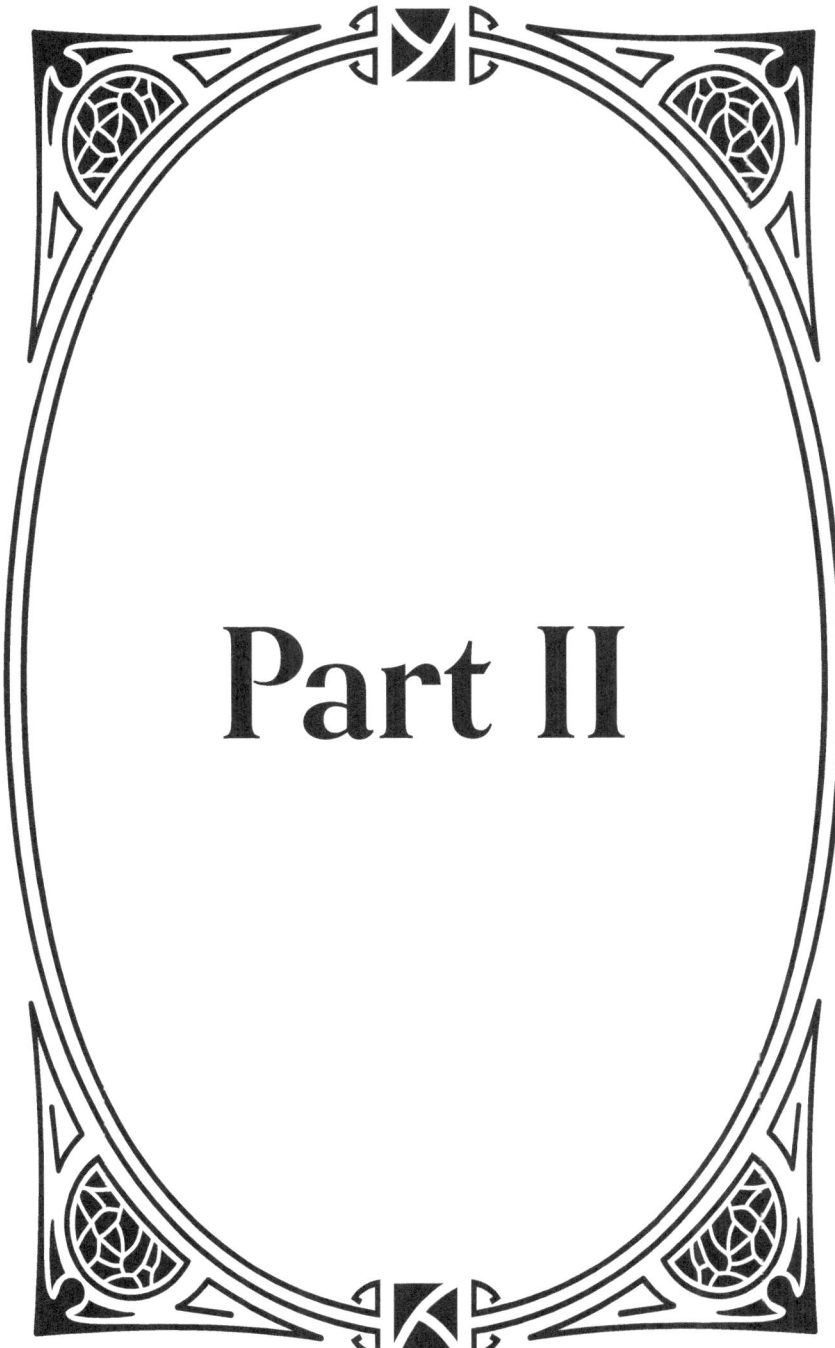

Part II

CHAPTER 29

1964 Boston

Bill Fitzgerald had just arrived home from his shift. His wife, Geri, had called him earlier in the day and told him she had heard from the adoption agency, and they were approved for adoption. He was pleased for her. They had been trying for years, and the wound festered. Being of the catholic faith, he knew how much having a family meant to Geri. Of course, he wanted a family too, but it was especially important to Geri. As he was driving home, a thought occurred to him: he would take her flowers. He knew she would love that. He stopped at the florist closest to their home.

"Oh, Bill, you are so sweet. They are lovely, thank you," she kissed him when he came in. "I'll go and get a vase to put these in."

"What are the options for the adoption?" he asked her when she returned to the family room. He could smell something good cooking in the kitchen.

"Marie told me there are several agencies in the Boston area. Then there was always the possibility of adopting from overseas."

"I would prefer adopting from within the country." He had known fellow officers who adopted from overseas, and the paperwork was endless. It was also expensive, especially if you had to fly abroad to meet the adoption agency and transport them home.

"I know that is your preference, and it is mine, also. But we're not getting any younger," Geri reminded him.

"What does that mean?"

"Just that if it drags on, I don't want to be *old* when I have a newborn."

"Does it have to be a newborn?" he asked her.

"I hadn't thought about adopting an older child. We never discussed it."

She was flustered at the thought of not adopting an infant. She had dreamed of holding an infant in her arms since she was a little girl. She grew up in a family with many aunts and uncles, each with numerous children. It was expected of their faith. She was the youngest of six and the only one who hadn't given birth.

"No, you're right. I'm sorry I brought it up. Just thinking out loud," Bill said, because he could see her disappointment.

"I think dinner is ready. I made a lasagna. Are you hungry?"

"Starved," he told her.

****

After dinner, Geri called her sister, Marie, and told her the news. She was very excited for her. She and Marie were very close in age. They were the 'Irish Twins' of the family, and they had a strong resemblance to each other.

"I'm so happy for you and Bill. Do you know how long it will take?"

"No, we have to wait; that is the hardest part. I'm ready to get the nursery ready. We purchased a crib at a yard sale about a year ago in hopes of my becoming pregnant, but of course, that never happened."

Marie could hear the sadness in her sister's voice. She knew Geri had a hard time discussing their infertility problems. Even though she deep down knew it wasn't Geri's fault, some people make hurtful comments.

"Are you still volunteering at the hospital?" asked Marie.

"Yes, I am in the nursery often. The nurses are so busy that they need help managing the turnover. The hospital lets mothers go home sooner than they used to; it is a common practice."

"I'm glad you stay busy with that. I'm sure you're still playing lots of tennis. You were the most athletic girl in our family."

"I'm still with the team that started last year. It's very competitive. We travel to other clubs to participate in games. It is a good exercise for me. You should take lessons, and we could play when we visit each other."

Marie and her family lived in North Carolina. Her husband was at Fort Bragg and was an Army officer. She was nervous about the day he would be deployed, with the war still raging in Vietnam. It will be his second tour. She has a six-month-old boy and two older girls, ages four and five.

"I hardly have time to get dressed during the day, Geri. You'll find out soon enough what it's like."

"I can't wait!" said Geri.

"I know, honey. I am praying for you."

"Thank you, I'd better go. I want to call Charlotte and Catherine."

"I understand. Thanks for letting me know. I'm here when you need to talk, okay?"

"Yes, I know."

CHAPTER
30

A month later, they received the call they were hoping for, but it was nothing like what they expected. It was a Sunday evening, and a friend of Bill's called to tell him a baby boy had been left at the local fire station. Andy knew how much Bill and Geri were looking forward to adopting.

The local parish priest somehow convinced the local Catholic charity that the Fitzgeralds would be perfect parents. They were already approved and had the means to bring an infant into their home. Within four days, Bill and Geri were bringing their infant son home. Family was there to greet them and showered them with gifts and love. It was an all-day celebration. Bill's precinct captain gave him a two-week leave of absence. They were on top of the world.

They chose the name Aaron. The name means 'mountain of strength' in Hebrew, and Aaron was Moses's brother, a well-known Biblical figure. He was given the middle name Gerald in honor of his maternal grandfather and his mother, who was named after her father.

Aaron was the apple of his parents' eyes. They couldn't have been happier with him. He was a good baby and grew into the cutest little boy. Since he was a foundling, they had no health history for him, but his pediatrician gave him a clean bill of health at each appointment. He was strong and smart. They delighted in how well coordinated he was and looked forward to the baseball and soccer games. He did not resemble either of them. Each had Irish roots and was fair-skinned. Bill had hazel eyes, and Geri had bright blue eyes. Bill's hair was dark brown, and Geri was more of a reddish blonde. Aaron was olive-skinned with brown eyes. He looked more Eastern European; they loved him with all their hearts.

Bill knew he wanted to rise through the police department, but it wasn't easy. His father was the chief before he retired. He had hoped to be promoted before now. They needed the extra income. Geri had started working part-time at Aaron's school as a teacher's aide. She didn't make much, but it helped.   He had begun searching for opportunities to transition into other areas, even if it meant relocating to another part of the country and leaving the Boston area. It would be a significant sacrifice for both of them, since their families were nearby, but he didn't want to continue without a promotion. His chances were bleak.

He discussed it with Geri, and she agreed, saying that if he were going to make a move, she would rather he did it while Aaron was still young. She wanted him to have a positive school experience. He already had friends who had known him since he started pre-school at their church, and it would be hard on him if they moved away. This request gave Bill the impetus to move soon.

He had a friend who lived in Binghamton, New York. He had moved there to work for the city as an engineer. They were neighbors a long time ago and kept in touch. He called him out of the blue one day and asked if he knew of any jobs for a chief of police. He told him he didn't mind if it was a small town. His friend told him he would put out some feelers and see what he could find out. He knew the chief of police in Binghamton, so he would ask for his help. Bill thanked him and hung up. He didn't think any more about it and continued to look in the trade papers for jobs. He was concerned that, since he had not held an administrative position, it would be challenging to transfer within the Boston area.

It was a Thursday, and Bill had taken the day off because it was Aaron's fifth birthday. They were having a pizza party for him that evening for his soccer buddies. Geri had been talking about finally telling Aaron that he was adopted. Bill wasn't sure he was ready. He loved his son so much, and he didn't want to let him know he was not of his flesh. He begged Geri to wait. She agreed, but said they should tell him by next year. Bill relented, knowing she was right. He was amazed Aaron hadn't asked or accidentally found out before now. He had cousins who knew he was adopted, but their parents asked them not to mention it until his parents told him. So far, so good.

Geri called him upstairs to say he had a phone call. He picked up the extension in the bedroom, and it was Mack, his friend in Binghamton.

"Bill, I think I have good news for you, if you are willing to move to New York."

"Tell me about it."

"There is a town not too far from Syracuse, called Eldridge. It is not very large, around twenty thousand, but growing. I think it is exactly what you are looking for. The Chief of Police is retiring, and they have been seeking a replacement. He would have retired long ago, but no one is ready to take his place. He is anxious. Are you interested?"

Bill wore a big smile. "I definitely am. Thank you."

"Here is a contact for you."

Bill wrote down the name and telephone number, assuring his friend he would call today. "This is Aaron's fifth birthday, so I took today off for the celebration. You have given me a gift, Mack. I am grateful."

He called the contact after he told Geri about the opportunity. She was a little put off about it being in New York; she was still hoping he would find something closer to Boston.

After a long conversation with the current chief, he worked on his resume and had it ready to mail before Aaron's party. He decided to take it to work the next day so he could make a copy, fax it to the chief, and then mail the original. He couldn't wait to get it to them.

CHAPTER
31

Bill traveled to Eldridge as soon as he could get time off from his current job. He felt the interview with the present Chief went well. Since he was in town for only two days, the Mayor and his Town Manager interviewed him the same day. They took him out to dinner that night, and they drove around the small town. He learned about the history of Eldridge. It was named after a Revolutionary War Hero, Thomas Eldridge. The city was founded when a group of settlers from the Northeast, primarily from Maine, moved in to stake a claim to the land. They were sold plots of land at low prices but were expected to farm them, and since they were farmers, it proved an easy assignment. Farmers were accustomed to working hard. They found the land fertile and built an irrigation system that endures to this day. Eventually, they had to choose a name, and since part of the Eldridge family had been instrumental in their fortunate move, they named their community Eldridge. That was in 1853, and things went well until the country went to war. Many of the sons joined the Union Army, and sadly, never came home. It hurt the community in many ways. The loss of life was devastating and caused a slowdown in the growth. As the older men fell ill and could no longer farm the land, the crops suffered. It took many years to rebuild it.

In 1877, the town announced that it needed young men to farm the land. They sent advertisements as far away as Rhode Island, Ohio, and North Carolina. The campaign apparently succeeded, as there was a sudden influx of men and families moving to the area. The cost of land was significantly reduced depending on its potential and whether it came with farm equipment. It took about five years, but Eldridge was buzzing with activity again. They became a large glass-factory town, with orders from all over the country. The railroad ran through their village, facilitating the shipment of goods.

Bill called Geri when he got back to the hotel and told her all about the town. He said he was confident an offer would come soon, and she should start collecting boxes to pack. Of course, they would need to put their house on the market. They couldn't afford to have two homes. They agreed that if needed, she would stay behind until Aaron was out for summer break. If the house were still unsold, they would need to consider renting it out. Bill didn't want to be a landlord. His father tried doing that, and it was disastrous. He got calls 24/7 until he had had enough and unloaded them for a song.

By the time he got back home, he had received a letter from the Chief offering him the position of Chief of Police. The Council approved his hiring after the Mayor and Town Manager gave him rave reviews. The salary could have been higher, but it wasn't bad. He felt they could find a house for a price comparable to what they were paying now, perhaps even less, since the cost of living was much lower than in Boston. He had discussed the average living expenses in Eldridge with the Chief and was pleased with what he was told.

He and Geri told Aaron when he got back from Eldridge. At first, he was upset about the move, but after they told him Eldridge had everything he needed there and that he would make friends easily, he felt better. He wanted to be the captain of everything.

Bill turned in his notice, and they contacted a real estate agent. She told them the prices of the homes comparable to theirs, and they were excited about the information. They knew they would have a sizeable down payment once their house sold. They agreed on a price, and the realtor got busy. She scheduled an Open House for the next two weeks. Geri knew she had to get busy to get the house in order. She was very excited. "I just wish I could have been there to see the town. Do you think we could drive over there one weekend?"

"Maybe. I hadn't thought about it. How about the weekend the realtor is having the open house?"

"That's a great idea," Geri told him.

That gave her the impetus to get busy. She was going to get Aaron involved as well. The garage needed cleaning out. In fact, she planned to have a yard sale. She would ask her sister for help.

****

Geri and Aaron worked hard on the house. At five years old, he was already very tall and could reach things with a ladder. He was athletic and strong for his age. They had the house ready for the Open House and were going to drive with Bill to Eldridge on Saturday.

"Mom, could I bring a friend?" asked Aaron.

Geri thought it over, and since Aaron had never asked for anything like that, she told him she would ask his father, considering it a great idea. "Who do you have in mind?"

"Tommy."

"Oh, okay. His mother will let him, you think?"

"I think so."

Geri felt sorry for Tommy. He was the same age as Aaron and was the youngest of six children. They've known each other since they were three, meeting at the park in their neighborhood. His mother, Judy, would bring Tommy to the park every morning. It was rumored that his father was an alcoholic, which didn't surprise her. Bill had told her he had seen him at the bars regularly. He knew he didn't make much money working for the transit company, driving a city bus. Aaron told her that one day, after they had been playing basketball outside, Tommy went to make them a sandwich but couldn't find the bread. Aaron made the mistake of opening the refrigerator and saw only a carton of eggs and a quart of milk. He told her he almost cried. Tommy was embarrassed, he could tell, but Aaron just said, "Let's go to my house. Your mom just hasn't had time to go to the store this week." Geri was proud of her son when he told her that story. From then on, Tommy was always welcome at their house for any meal. She knew Aaron would miss him, and so would she.

That night, Bill told Aaron it was okay to take Tommy. They planned to get up early on Saturday and leave, so Tommy would stay at their house on Friday night. Geri called Tommy's mother and gave her all of their travel information, in case of an emergency. She learned Tommy tended to be car sick, so she was going to send along the medicine their doctor prescribed. Geri told her she would make sure he took it.

CHAPTER
32

They arrived in Eldridge around three o'clock. Bill knew there was a Holiday Inn near the police station, so they stopped and booked a room. After that, he took them to the police station and showed them around. Since it was Saturday, there was a skeleton crew. It was slow on a Saturday afternoon. He met the officers on duty and told them he was looking forward to working with them. They were professional and helpful, making him feel welcome. It made the trip worthwhile. He asked the officers if they could recommend a real estate company that would help them find a place. Officer Nat Kendrick gave him the name Andrews Realty and directions. He thanked them and told them he looked forward to being there in a couple of weeks. He had given a month's notice as was customary in his profession.

They decided to visit Andrews Realty before closing, then go out to eat. The boys agreed they could wait. They had a big lunch at McDonald's on the way there.

There was only one employee in the agency when they arrived. She introduced herself as Maureen Andrews and said she was a co-owner with her brother, Michael. After talking with them for a while, she asked about their budget.

Geri said, "It's hard to say, but we should have a sizeable down payment if everything goes well with our house sale. What are the average prices for a three-bedroom, one and a half to two bathrooms?"

"We will be able to find you a lovely home in the low forties. How does that sound?"

Geri looked at Bill, and he shrugged. "I would like to see a variety in that price range. Do you have any in mind? We are here until tomorrow. We will need to leave around eleven to get home in time for Bill to go to work on Monday."

"Sure, I can get a couple together. Would you be willing to view one today? I know it is getting late, but I have one that is empty, so that it wouldn't be a problem. We could go at any hour."

Bill said, "That would be great. We cannot put an offer in until we sell our house, but if we love it, maybe we could work something out?"

"You'll find in Eldridge, the people are easy-going, and I believe we can work with you. We have been in business here for over forty years. Michael and I took the business over ten years ago when our parents retired and moved to Florida."

"I hope it was the plan for you and your brother to take it over all along," said Geri.

"Yes, we knew we would inherit the business. We were prepared. Also, my parents made an offer we couldn't refuse. The only thing they asked for was a monthly salary from the business, enough to keep a roof over their heads in Florida. So they are living well," she laughed.

"Why don't you all drive around Eldridge, perhaps get a bite to eat, and then let's meet up here about six. That is when I will close the agency, and we'll go look at the house I have in mind."

Bill said, "Sounds good. We can check with the motel to see if they have a sitter available for the boys. We are staying at the Holiday Inn near the police station."

"Good choice. I'll give you a voucher for a room discount. We help people out when they come in town to do research on relocating and have a reciprocal agreement with most of the motels."

"Great, I like it here more and more."

****

The front desk clerk handed Bill a list of babysitter names and assured him they had been vetted. When Bill went back to the car, he gave it to Geri, and she began calling the names on the list after they reached their room. She got in touch with the second on the list, who said she was free that evening. Geri gave her their room number, and the woman told her she would see her a little before six. Both boys had brought their own toy, and Geri threw in a Monopoly Game at the last minute. That should keep them busy, Geri and Bill hoped. They left to take the boys to dinner, and while out, they toured the downtown. They found a few stores in the town square that looked interesting, but they were closed for the day. They also found two churches that looked promising. They attended a Methodist church back home, so it would make sense to transfer to one here. They left the Catholic church after they adopted Aaron because of the church's stance on birth control. Geri was a progressive at heart, and she felt the church did not fulfill her more contemporary beliefs. Geri's family was not pleased about it, but it was what they wanted. Besides, the Methodist church was the next best thing. The boys wanted to eat at a nice restaurant, so they found a seafood place and seemed satisfied. After a good dinner and being all stuffed, they returned the boys to the motel. The babysitter, Mrs. Turner, arrived shortly after.

They arrived at the realty company about five minutes early. Maureen came out a few minutes later and directed them to her car, a very nice Mercedes. She was very smartly dressed in a black pantsuit and white blouse. She was petite, with black hair cut stylishly. It made her face very attractive. Geri wondered if she should get a new hairdo. She had worn her hair the same way for years. She made up her mind that she definitely could use a makeover.

They drove to the house, set in a secluded subdivision outside of town.

"This is a newer neighborhood, and they have excellent schools. I think you'll be pleased. The house is empty only because the owner was transferred and the company purchased the home."

When Maureen drove into the driveway, Geri could tell it was going to be a winner. They noticed the detail as they approached the front door. It had a lovely porch and was all brick. The shutters were colonial blue, a color very popular at the time.

It had three large bedrooms, the master the largest, and its own bathroom. There was another large bathroom across from the other two bedrooms. Geri wondered if they might be able to adopt another child, with all of this room.

Bill fell in love with the backyard and deck. It was spacious, with ample room for a grill, a table, and chairs. He noticed how thick the grass was with very few weeds. He enjoyed a manicured yard and thought he might get a riding lawn mower if they could afford it. Geri walked out on the porch and said, "I know you like this deck. Oh, Bill, why did we have to find this house first? I want to move in it now!"

He pulled her to him and kissed her on her forehead. "I know what you mean."

Maureen walked out and asked how they liked it.

Geri admitted she was in love. The kitchen was perfect. Everything was updated. The refrigerator came with the house, which was fine with her because theirs back home was about ready to die. She hoped it would last until they sold the house.

"Are you ready for the price?" asked Maureen.

"Lay it on me," said Bill.

"39,800 is the asking. It is lower than the prices of other homes. Because the home had been empty for forty-five days, the company is ready to sell. The homes in this subdivision go as high as $46,000."

Geri and Bill looked at each other.

"How long do you think we can wait?"

"It's hard to say," Maureen said.

"I may be able to hold for thirty days with a good-faith deposit. Probably $500 would do it, and it would go toward your down payment."

"Let us sleep on it tonight," said Geri. "I've got to wrap my head around everything, and we need to discuss our budget. I hope you understand."

"Of course, I will pick you up at the Holiday Inn tomorrow morning at nine o'clock. We'll look at a couple more. They are not far from my office."

"Sounds good," said Bill.

When they returned to the motel, they found the boys asleep on one of the double beds, and Mrs. Turner was reading a magazine. She told them they were no trouble. Bill paid her, giving her a generous tip. She thanked him and left.

"What do you think, hon?" asked Bill.

"I loved the house. We'll see what she shows us tomorrow, but it's going to take a lot to compete with the one we saw tonight."

CHAPTER
33

Their realtor picked all of them up promptly at nine o'clock. Bill insisted on following her since they had the boys. Geri rode in Maureen's Mercedes. She showed them three homes. Two were in the same neighborhood, and one was in another subdivision, not far from the one they visited the previous day.

Geri didn't like the two that were close together because the kitchens badly needed an upgrade. Bill didn't like the other house because it didn't have a back deck; it only had a concrete patio.

"Well, what do you think?" asked Maureen after they pulled into a McDonald's to eat.

Bill and Geri looked at each other and said, "We would like to put a deposit on the house you showed us yesterday."

"Great, I thought you were going to say that, so I have paperwork ready to go. If you would give me a deposit of $500 today, I will see if the owner, which, as I mentioned, is a corporation, will agree to remove it from the market for thirty days. Will that give you enough time to get your house sold?"

Geri said, "I think so. It's on the market now, and there was an Open House while we were here."

"That sounds promising."

Bill handed Maureen a check. "Well, I think that takes care of our business here. Let's eat."

The boys went to the counter to order with Bill while Geri hung back. "What is Eldridge like?" she asked Maureen.

"It is a quiet town with very kind and down-to-earth people. Bill should do great as our new Chief. Are you planning on working?"

"I don't know yet. Once Aaron is settled in school, I might look for part-time work. I want to be home with him in the afternoons. I would like to meet new people and cultivate new hobbies. Any tennis courts nearby?"

"I understand, and yes, there is a very nice country club that I think you would enjoy. They have a golf course, swimming pool, and all of the amenities. You would get to know people fast there."

"Thanks, I'll look into that."

Bill returned with the food, and they ate their lunches while answering all of the boy's questions.

****

After finishing their meal, they returned to the motel, checked out, and headed home. The boys were excited about another road trip, but fell fast asleep shortly after they left. Geri thought the food and Tommy's medicine had made him sleepy, and Aaron fell asleep easily anyway. She guessed they were tired out from the ride there as well. He and Geri discussed the move, including whether they could sell their house soon and secure a loan in Eldridge. He knew their credit was good and they should have a nice-sized down payment. They both agreed they had a lot to do when they got back to move on the house they wanted.

After crossing into Vermont, they stopped at a small diner and got a late lunch. By then, the boys were awake and hungry. The rest of the trip was uneventful. They dropped Tommy off at his home around five o'clock. He was glad to see his mom. He thanked Bill and Geri for taking him on the trip. Geri thought it was endearing how Tommy had such a sweet nature. She wished he had a better home life.

The following morning, Geri called their realtor to see how the open house went. They saw the flyers on the front hall table when they arrived home. There were a few business cards from other realtors who were likely scouting their home for potential buyers.

The phone rang a couple of times, then a pleasant voice answered, "Canton Realty, how may I help you?"

Geri asked, "Is Marie Sharpe available?"

"Hold please."

"Hello, this is Marie."

"Marie, this is Geri Fitzgerald. We were wondering how the open house went."

"I'm so glad you called. It went great. There was a lot of interest, and I have four people who want to come back out this week if that is okay with you."

"Absolutely, just let us know when, and we will make sure we are out of the house. I will keep it in order in the meantime, which is quite a feat with Aaron around," she laughed.

"No problem. I believe one will be this afternoon at four o'clock."

"Great, I will let Bill know, and Aaron and I will leave just before then. Just let me know if anything changes, okay?"

"I will, thank you. I am anticipating a bidding war on your house, which is unheard of these days."

"I like the sound of that," said Geri.

She called Bill to inform him about today's events and the brewing bidding war. "I am so excited, now. I'm ready to start decorating our new home!"

Bill was happy for her. They spent their entire lives in Massachusetts, and he felt they could use a fresh start. Aaron had not yet started school to avoid making it too much of an interruption in his life. He wanted to advance in his career, and starting anew in a new town would benefit him. He loved what he did, and he felt he could make a significant impact at a smaller police force.

That evening, the realtor called them to say the couple who had looked at it that afternoon had made an offer. However, she received another call from a realtor whose client, who had looked at it on Saturday, also wanted to make an offer. She was waiting for the client's decision. She said she would call them the next day, hopefully with an offer at their asking price.

The following afternoon, Marie called Geri to say she had three offers and would come by that evening to go over them. Geri agreed, and they decided on seven o'clock, because Bill will be home by then.

At seven, Marie arrived, and Bill greeted her. They sat at their kitchen table, and Marie pulled all of the proposed offers out of her attaché.

They all had some provisions attached, but the cleanest and most promising came from a couple who already lived in a Boston suburb and were currently renting. They were anxious to move because their lease was about to expire. His parents were buying the home in cash, so there wouldn't be a financing delay. Apparently, their son had just graduated from law school and was taking a position at a prestigious Boston law firm, but he didn't want his wife and two children to live in the city. They felt the schools in their area were excellent and wanted their children to attend the local school system.

Bill and Geri talked it over, and it wasn't long before they agreed to accept their offer. It was their asking price, and the closing would be as soon as possible.

After signing all of the paperwork, they were drained and celebrated with a bottle of wine. They were not heavy drinkers, but this was a time to unwind. Aaron heard all the excitement and came into the kitchen to see what it was all about. They told him they would be moving to the town they had just visited. He was excited yet sad to leave his friend, Tommy. Geri assured him that Tommy could visit him anytime.

CHAPTER 34

Geri and Gloria Malcom had just come off the tennis courts and were planning on meeting their friends in the club's lounge and having lunch.

They had been tennis partners for a while, since Geri moved to Eldridge. Their friendship began when Geri attended a Tupperware party at a neighbor's house and met Gloria there. They bonded over their love for tennis.

As she removed her bra, Geri felt the lump again. She first noticed it three days ago, but hoped it would go away. Now, she was concerned and thought she should have it checked out. She had not sought out an OBGYN since moving to Eldridge. They only had a family doctor, whom she took Aaron to.

"Gloria, would you come here a minute?"

Gloria walked over to her friend, who had a towel covering her breasts. She turned so that Gloria was facing her left side. "Would you feel right here and tell me if you feel anything?"

"Okay, what am I feeling for?"

"I think a lump."

Gloria felt the skin and pressed where Geri indicated. She immediately removed her hand and said, "Geri, you need to get that looked at. There is a lump there, no doubt. Do you need a doctor referral? I have a very good OBGYN."

"I'll take that name, yes. I should have found one when I moved here. It took forever to get a general practitioner."

"I know what you mean, they are getting more and more scarce."

Gloria wrote down her doctor's name and said she should be able to find the number easily in the phone book. "He will take good care of you. Tell them I recommended them to you."

"I will."

****

Geri called the OBGYN, Dr. Rosenthal, as soon as she got home. She was very nervous about the lump now that Gloria had felt it. She hadn't told Bill yet. They scheduled an appointment for her later in the week.

When Bill got home that night, she told him about her appointment with the doctor Gloria had recommended.

"Good, you should see a regular doctor, Geri. I need to set up another appointment. The department wants me to have regular check-ups. It is in my contract."

She arrived at Dr. Rosenthal's office early and sat in the car praying. Her mother had passed away when she was only twelve years old in a car accident. She had never known her grandmother on her mother's side because she had died before she was born, and she wasn't sure what she died of. There was talk of some influenza back then, and she must have caught it. There wasn't much money, so they didn't go to the doctor for even minor issues. She passed away, and no one ever knew why, or at least not that she heard.

Dr. Rosenthal was very nice. He had a head full of gray hair and dark eyebrows. His facial features were strong, and his dark brown eyes bored a hole through you. It was stark, mainly because of how nice his demeanor was.

He checked her breast and noted the lump she had pointed out.

"We will need to get a mammogram scan of your breast and remove fluid. I want to set that up this afternoon. Is that okay?"

"Yes, of course," she almost stuttered, shocked by his urgency.

"Patsy, would you get that set up STAT and if need be, cancel my appointments in the office?"

"Yes, sir, I will."

He finished the exam, checking her uterus and performing a pap smear.

When she was dressed, Patsy, his nurse, came back in with instructions on where to go and the time. "No deodorant or creams, okay?"

"Of course," said Geri.

She rushed home and called Bill. He was out on a case and was told they would get the message to him so he could call her. She then called Gloria.

****

Gloria picked her up to go to the hospital. She had to call John, her husband, to arrange to pick up the children from their schools. He was a pharmacist, and he had an assistant who could cover for him for a short time. He told her he would bring the kids, Janet, and Craig, back to the store.

When they arrived at the hospital's radiology department, Bill was waiting there. Gloria thought he looked rightfully concerned. She didn't know Bill very well, as they hadn't been out socially. She was very close to Geri because of their shared love of tennis.

Bill stood and hugged Geri, and she began to cry. They sat across from Gloria, and she saw how deeply in love they were with each other. She wondered if her husband would be so attentive. She and John had not been as close in the last few years because of his work hours and all the children's activities.

Once they took Geri back for the procedure, she and Bill sat and talked like old friends. They got to know each other better during that hour of waiting. He was old school when it came to policing. He believed in discipline but not in a harsh manner. He told her his father had been a harsh disciplinarian, and he never wanted to be that way. "The Greatest Generation, if you know what I mean," he told her. She understood that his father had fought in World War II and was probably a stoic. Gloria had been raised as an only child and didn't need much discipline. She was very close to her mother and was easy to raise. She was lucky with her two children as well. They were both easy-going, and motherhood came naturally to her. John left everything up to her. He had wanted more children, but she had enough on her hands and discouraged it. She wonders if that was the rift between them.

The doctor came out and spoke with Bill. He took him aside into a conference room, and when he came out, he looked shaken.

"He believes it is cancer. He is scheduling her to have a mastectomy, pending the pathology results."

Gloria hung her head and began to cry. "I am so sorry. Anything I can do to help out, please let me know."

He looked at her long and hard, then said, "I will, thank you."

Gloria looked up and smiled at him, "Anything at all, Bill?"

****

A week later, the results were back, and Geri's lump was malignant. Surgery was scheduled for the following week with another doctor. She went to see him, and he explained to her and Bill what he would do. She went in on a Wednesday morning. The plan was to check for lymph node malignancy; however, the surgeon had already told them that he believed, due to the size of the lump, that it was aggressive, and he expected to be doing a full mastectomy of the left breast, including lymph nodes.

"How long will the surgery be?" asked Geri.

"I usually say 'as long as it needs to be, ' but I will just tell you approximately four hours, maybe longer," he said. He could see the fright in his patient's eyes.

"Thank you, Dr. Stephens."

When they arrived on Wednesday morning, Gloria was there. She waited in the waiting room for Bill to come out and sit with her. They said very little for the first hour, then both agreed to get a cup of coffee.

"Where are your children?"

"School. I arranged with a neighbor to have them go to her house if I'm not home. She's going to look out for them. John couldn't get out of work. His assistant had classes today and couldn't come in. It is what it is."

"Well, thank you. You are a great friend to Geri. And me," he added.

"You're welcome."

CHAPTER
35

When Geri was moved to a room, Bill and Gloria were there to meet her. The surgeon was right about the time it would take. She had to spend extra time in the recovery room because she had a difficult time waking up.

"Hi, sweetheart," Bill reached down and kissed her lips.

Gloria was on the other side of the bed, but she stepped away to give them a moment. After a couple of minutes, Bill stepped away, and she went up to the siderail and took Geri's hand. "I'm here, Geri."

Geri looked over at Gloria with tears in her eyes. "I'm so sorry, but you're going to have to get another tennis partner."

Gloria burst out laughing. "You 'ole teaser, I hope you're not serious!"

"I am, Gloria. I don't see myself getting back to it anytime soon."

"I'm not worried about it one bit. You'll get well, and we'll be out there again."

Unfortunately, Gloria was wrong. Geri was never able to play tennis again.

****

She went home after three days and arranged for home health care to help her bathe and change dressings. The first time she saw her incision over where her left breast should be, the nurse was with her. She touched the area tenderly, and tears began to flow. It wasn't the nurse's first time being with a patient when she realized she no longer had the breast she had had all of her life. The nurse had seen the entire gamut of emotions. Some took it in stride, but others, including Geri, mourned the loss.

She learned that she had four lymph nodes removed and would have to learn how to prevent lymphedema. These were medical terms she had never heard of. The nurse showed her a few exercises to start controlling the swelling of her left arm. She left her some paperwork to remind her what to do.

She had her first shower since surgery, washing her hair. She had it cut short just before surgery, as recommended by some literature she had read in the surgeon's office. The nurse helped her dress and suggested she not wear anything buttoned up for a while. "You'll be fitted for a prosthetic which will help balance you, so don't worry about how you look right now. You'll see a significant difference in how you look after the prosthesis is fitted."

Geri wanted to cry again, but she held back, feeling she had put her nurse through enough this visit. After the nurse left, she sat at the kitchen table and cried. Then she got up and managed to heat the soup Gloria had made for her. She had been such a good friend. She didn't know what she would have done without her.

She was referred to an oncologist and was to meet with him the following Monday. Bill had arranged to get off of work and take her. She also had made an appointment, as recommended, with a wig company in the next town over. The Cancer Society contacted her with the woman's name and number. The wigs are made free of charge and, from what she has learned, are made from real hair donated through hair salons. Her hair was a light brown with reddish highlights. She dreaded when she would start losing her hair.

The oncologist recommended that she start chemotherapy only a week later. Geri was reluctant, but Bill insisted she follow the doctor's recommendation. She just wasn't ready for the nausea, which she knew about, and the loss of her hair. But with his encouragement, they agreed on the date and time.

Gloria took her to the wig place the next day. They actually had fun browsing through all the styles, and she ended up choosing a color close to hers, but in a style different from what she was used to. "What the heck," she told Geri, "I might as well remake my whole self." She was referring to the loss of her breast, but she wasn't sure if Gloria had picked up on it.

They found a restaurant and ate lunch. Geri tried to keep the conversation light. After lunch, they did some shopping at the J. C. Penney in a nearby mall, where Geri bought pullover tops with high necklines. She had not yet looked into the prosthesis. She was told to ensure the incision site was well-healed and free of edema. Fitting the bra was paramount to the prosthesis's fit.

They got back to Eldridge before three o'clock, and in time for the school bus. After dropping Geri off at her home, Gloria drove home to wait for the kids. Janet had cheerleading practice that afternoon, and Craig had Little League practice. Somehow, she would need to figure out what they were having for dinner. She chided herself for thinking that was a 'problem' with all that Geri had to face.

She called John at the pharmacy to see how his day had been, and he told her, "It's been busy."

"Okay, just checking in. What do you want for dinner? I have to take Janet to cheer practice, and Craig has little league practice."

"Anything you want to do. I'm not picky." She knew that was true. John would eat anything. She decided to take out the frozen vegetable soup she had made a week ago so that she could give Geri some. She figured it would thaw if she put it in some hot water now. She liked her new microwave, but didn't trust it to thaw. Her friend ruined a steak by thawing it in her microwave.

That night after dinner, Janet went up to do her homework, and John sat at the kitchen table to help Craig with his. She worked in the kitchen, cleaning it up and preparing breakfast the next morning. She liked to send the kids off with a hot breakfast when she had time, but lately it was getting hard to do. She decided to cook the bacon so it would be ready to reheat in the morning. That was one thing she did like about her microwave.

CHAPTER
36

Two months later

Geri had just returned home after her eighteenth chemotherapy session. Glora took her there today. In fact, Gloria took her to every other one, trading off with Bill. Her sister, Grace, came in town for the first two weeks of her treatment, which was very nice. They didn't get to spend much time together, and Geri hated that she had to spend her visit taking her for treatments. However, as a neonatal nurse, she could explain medical procedures to Geri.

Geri had lost weight during these weeks; in fact, she was down thirty pounds from her highest weight of one thirty-five. She felt like a bag of bones. Her skin pallor was pale, slightly gray. She studied herself in the mirror and could see how her health was deteriorating. Her norm was make-up, lipstick, and hair always in place. Nowadays, she can barely run a brush through her wig. Most of the time, she only wears the scarf that Bill bought at Maxine's, an upscale ladies' store in town.

Aaron was always so quiet around her. He didn't want to disturb her in any way. She wished he wouldn't be so timid. It made her sad, and she feared he would never forget her like this. He was due home from school any minute, so she changed into something he wouldn't expect: jeans and a sweater. The jeans camouflaged her weight. The large sweater helped, too. She put her wig in place and added a touch of blush and lipstick to give herself some color.

She went into the kitchen and pulled out the cookies Geri had given her to share with Aaron. Geri had been such a good friend during these past few months. She knew she didn't feel like baking cookies, so she made sure there were some for Aaron, just as her own kids liked to come home to freshly baked cookies.

****

That night, she woke up in a sweat. She felt like she had broken a fever. She didn't feel feverish when she went to bed, so she was disturbed at this sudden change. She went to their bathroom and removed her gown. She stepped into a lukewarm bath and let it envelop her in a soothing balm. Her chills stopped. She started getting sleepy again, and before she almost drifted off, she decided she'd better get out of the tub and put on a clean gown.

She crawled back into the bed. Bill rolled over and looked at her. She thought he was awake, but wasn't sure. He began to cough and had to sit up to stop. "Do you want me to get you some water, hon?"

"No, that's okay. I'll go into the kitchen. Do you want anything?"

"No, I'm fine," she lied.

She watched as her six-foot, muscular husband walked toward the bedroom door. She missed making love to him. She missed a lot of things.

She had an appointment with her oncologist the next day. She insisted to Bill that she would drive herself. At the appointment, she was told she had completed her treatments, which she already knew. She was told to go on about her lifestyle as she wished. No restrictions. She asked about her weight loss. The doctor said to her that now that the treatment was complete, she would regain most of her weight.

Afterward, she went to Baskin-Robbins and had a Banana Split. She ate every bite and vowed to go at least once a week until her weight increased significantly.

She had a follow-up appointment with the oncologist scheduled for three months later; however, she had developed a cough, and one morning she coughed up blood. Bill insisted she call the oncologist and make an appointment.

"I'm not worried about the lung," the oncologist said. It doesn't appear to be cause for concern, but we found a lesion on your liver. There is nothing we can do but see if it grows. Sometimes these are nothing, and right now, the area is too small to take a biopsy. I would like to see you back in thirty days, and then we will get another X-ray. If it hasn't grown, it is probably nothing, but if it has, we will decide on the next steps."

They left there in a depressed state, but Geri tried to lift the mood by talking about wanting to have a garden in the spring.

"You mean a flower garden?" asked Bill.

"No, I mean a vegetable garden."

"Okay, let's do it. You pick the spot, and I will get it tilled. We'll have to put up a fence around it to keep the deer and other pesky animals out."

"True, why don't we fence in the yard. Aaron has been wanting a dog. We could adopt one from the shelter."

"Great idea. Let's check the costs. Would you look into it?" he asked.

"Yes, I will."

It was the first time he had seen her smile in quite a while.

That night, they told Aaron they were considering fencing in the yard, and once that was done, they would start looking for a dog.

"Really?" he asked.

"Yes, really." Geri smiled at how excited he was. There had been so much gloom and doom around her illness, and she felt guilty about it. She wanted so badly to do something for her son that he would remember for a long time.

The next day, she started calling fencing companies and made appointments for them to come out for an estimate. That evening, she told Bill about the appointments and had asked that they provide written estimates. He was glad she had something to occupy her time.

****

By the following week, they had received three estimates: two for a chain-link fence and one for an iron fence painted white. They knew the chain-link wall would be cheaper, but the look of the iron-white fence was much nicer. They wanted to maintain the neighborhood's look and noticed that more neighbors had the iron style. They made a nice profit on the home they sold in Massachusetts and knew they could afford a nicer-looking fence.

"Are we in agreement? The white fence?" asked Bill.

Geri laughed. "Yes, the white picket fence. She kissed Bill on the cheek. In turn, he pinched her rear. "Oooh!" she cried out, smiling.

"I'll call them tomorrow and get it scheduled. Aaron will be so excited."

****

The fence was installed, and Geri had taken Aaron to the shelter, where he picked out a mixed-breed, mostly German Sheppard. It was part of a litter dropped off a week ago. They were only about six weeks old, according to the staff. It was what Aaron wanted, so she called Bill, and he agreed it would be good to start with a young pup so they could train him right.

The shelter staff informed her that the puppy had undergone a vet check-up and was dewormed, but would require shots soon. She asked about a veterinarian and was given a name. She called when they got home and made the appointment. Aaron was so excited about having the puppy in the car that she could hardly drive. When they got home, he was ready to test names. "Why don't you wait until your dad gets home, and we will all decide together?"

"Okay"

Bill was home early because he couldn't wait to see the puppy. He had stopped by the pet store and picked up bedding, dog bowls, and puppy food.

"Hey there, little buddy," Bill said to the puppy as it was jumping up and down. Aaron was on the floor rolling around with him.

"Dad, we need to name him. Mom told me we were to wait for you to get home so you could help us. What do you think?"

"What do you want to name him?" asked Bill.

"I think Buddy?"

"I like it, but what about something else. We'll nickname him Buddy, how about that?"

"What about George?" asked Aaron.

"What about Ranger?" asked Geri. She was listening to this exchange from the kitchen.

Aaron looked at his dad and said, "I like it."

Bill said, "Ranger, it sounds good. It's up to you."

"Ranger," Aaron looked at the dog. The dog turned his head back and forth like he was trying to understand.

Bill laughed, "I think he likes it."

CHAPTER
37

A month had passed, and it was time for Geri to have another test, this time on her liver. The office called and gave her the appointment date and time. Bill went with her, and they were both nervous.

She underwent the X-ray, and they went back home to spend the afternoon alone. Geri had wanted to talk with Bill about their future. She began to accept that her life was likely to be cut short. When she told him they needed to talk about arrangements for when she passed, he said he couldn't discuss it. She begged him. It had taken all the energy she had to be able to bring it up, and she didn't think she could do it again. She was surprised at his attitude.

She dropped the subject, not wanting to ruin their time alone. She went out to her newly tilled garden and planned where to plant. The weather was still too cool for planting, but she wanted to be ready in case she didn't have the energy to show Bill where to plant.

The puppy was very active. They let him stay inside for now because of his size. They were afraid he would slip through the fence. He needed to bulk up so he wouldn't be able to get through it. She was so glad they had adopted the puppy. It was the best thing to happen to Aaron in a long time.

Geri busied herself with doing some pre-spring cleaning. She had put off some things during the time she received chemo. She washed the bathroom curtains and thoroughly cleaned Aaron's room. She found wrappers under his bed, which were from the candy she kept in the den. She didn't like him having too much because of his teeth, and she also didn't want him to gain weight. She had noticed how many kids were staying inside, watching TV instead of playing outside, riding bikes, or playing with their pets. It was a much different era than when she and Bill grew up. She encouraged him to play sports and engage in regular physical activity. Ranger had helped him get outside more. It was his responsibility to take Ranger for a walk when he arrived home from school. She was also teaching him how much food to prepare for the dog. She knew one day she would not be there, and she was trying to prepare her son for that eventuality.

The phone rang while she was cleaning out the refrigerator. It was the doctor's office, and they wanted her to schedule an appointment for the next day. She called Bill and told him so he could arrange to go with her.

The following day, she and Bill sat nervously in the office. They would find out what the X-ray showed. Geri wasn't ready for it. She knew in her heart of hearts the news wouldn't be good.

Finally, her name was called, and they were led back to a room. The doctor came in and gave them the news. The lesion had grown, and they found two more lesions nearby. She was scheduled for a biopsy the following week.

The biopsy came back showing malignant cells. The cancer had spread. He told them how sorry he was to deliver this news.

"We can restart the chemotherapy. It will be a different regimen, but it might be successful." He told them he could not make promises, but he would recommend trying it.

Geri said, "I'd like to have a few days to think about it."

Dr. Shaffer said, "That's fine, but please don't take too long. Your chances of success decrease every day."

That statement jarred Bill. He reached over and took Geri's hand. They left shortly after and were quiet all the way home.

"I'd like to speak with our minister, Bill. Would you call Pastor Robertson and make an appointment for me?"

"Of course."

✶✶✶✶✶✶✶✶✶✶✶✶

Pastor Robertson came by that evening and sat with Geri in their living room. They prayed for her decisions to be what God wanted. They also prayed for Bill and Aaron. She stressed that they would need strength to face the inevitable. She told the pastor she would decide her fate in a few days and promised to let him know. He left her with several Bible passages and a brochure on planning a Christian burial. She thanked him for his time and healing words. He went quietly, leaving her to contemplate how she would tell Bill her decision.

✶✶✶✶✶✶✶✶✶

Gloria met Geri at the club the following day, and Geri told her she had decided she wasn't going to continue chemotherapy. Gloria didn't know what to say. She respected her friend's decision, but she knew she had a very difficult time ahead. Geri watched her grandfather deteriorate and suffer in pain when he had colon cancer. It was a long time ago; however, she could still remember his screams. He was medicated with morphine and spent the last month of his life basically comatose. Her grandmother kept him at home and nursed him, leaving his side only to make him tea and tend to her basic needs. It was hard for her mother to watch her father suffer, and she coddled Gloria during this time.

One day she came home from school, only to find out her grandfather had passed away and was out of his pain. She always thought how paradoxical. He had to die to get rid of the pain. It was indelibly imprinted on her heart how much her grandmother suffered during that time. She was never the same after that.

Geri said, "Gloria, you have been the best friend. I couldn't have made it without you. Please take care of Bill and Aaron. I appreciate you welcoming Aaron into your home to play with Craig, and I hope they will remain friends."

"You don't have to be concerned about that, Geri. I love Aaron like a son. He will always be welcome. I love you so much, you're the sister I never had."

"We have had some fun times. Keep playing tennis and remember how hard we tried to win that club trophy. I thought sooner or later we would win it."

Gloria laughed. "I know, it would have been cool. Just remembering how competitive we were and how much we enjoyed those times will keep me going."

"Let's order lunch, I'm hungry," said Geri.

CHAPTER

38

Geri passed away at home on Christmas Eve of 1970. Once she decided not to continue chemotherapy, it was a relief for her. She did well for three months, but then started having symptoms. She was in pain from bone cancer. They learned it had metastasized to the bone, and it was all downhill from there. She was placed in hospice after Thanksgiving and slipped into a coma a week before Christmas.

Gloria kept Aaron during Christmas break so that Bill could be with Geri. They even brought Ranger to their home, and Aaron and Craig took turns caring for him. One would be the walker, and the other would make sure he was fed. It was a new experience to have a dog around. Janet even got into the act. She insisted Ranger loved to sleep in her room and would take his bed there every night. Aaron relented since he was the guest and thought she needed to feel like she was helping him. Aaron grew into his own during that time and reached a maturity not typically found in a seven-year-old.

Her funeral was on New Year's Eve at the Methodist Church. Afterward, she was transferred to Boston and buried in the family cemetery there. There was a small graveside service held there for the family that could not come to Eldridge for services.

Gloria grieved her friend. John tried to be sympathetic, but he didn't understand how sad she had been during Geri's illness. He was raised by a family that wasn't close. His father passed away while he was in college, before he met Gloria. After they married, his mother lived with them for a few years until Janet was born, then they moved her to a nursing home. By this time, she had developed Alzheimer's, and Gloria couldn't handle a newborn and her mother-in-law. John understood. He had two brothers, but neither offered to help. He resented them for years afterward. Once his mother was in the nursing home, they would visit her every Sunday. She passed away on Janet's first birthday. John knew it was a blessing. She never knew her granddaughter.

One day, she was home alone, writing letters, when the doorbell rang, unexpectedly. She looked through the peephole and saw Bill Fitzgerald standing there. She naturally opened the door and invited him in.

"Hi, Gloria. I was in the neighborhood and thought I would stop in. I hope I'm not interrupting anything."

"No, you're not. Come on in, and I'll make you a cup of coffee."

They went into the kitchen, and he sat at the kitchen table. She went to get cups from the cupboard, and when she turned around, she saw him with his head in his hands, crying.

She went over and wrapped her arm around his shoulder. He kept his head down. "I know, Bill. I miss her, too."

"I don't know what I am going to do, Gloria. I am lost without her. We were so close. I don't know how God could do this to us."

"I know you don't mean that."

"No, I'm not mad at God. I'm just a weak person. I don't have the strength Geri had."

Gloria set a cup of coffee in front of Bill. "Here, this should make you feel better."

Bill reached for her wrist and looked up into her eyes, tears in them.

She felt very uncomfortable at that moment. It crossed her mind that Bill was making a pass at her. She didn't know what to do.

She sat across from him while he sipped his coffee. He finally let her wrist go and apologized.

"That's okay, really. I have wept almost every day, Bill. You had a wonderful wife, and you are in a bad place right now. But you'll get past it. This is the time for you to be strong, especially for Aaron."

He started nodding his head. He wiped his eyes, and she reached for a Kleenex to give to him. When she did, he took her hand and held it. At that moment, she knew what he wanted, and she knew what was going to happen. She had never even considered cheating on her husband. She read her share of trashy novels. She wasn't proud of it, but she was attracted to Bill. She had been ever since they moved here. She was even jealous of Geri for having such a handsome husband. Bill was tall with dark hair and strong facial features. He was muscular and could have been a model on the front cover of some of those trashy novels. This was the moment of no return. She reached down and kissed him on the mouth. His lips were very soft, and he was a great kisser.

He pulled away and stood up. I'm sorry, Gloria. I shouldn't have come. He turned and walked to the front door. She wasn't sure if she should follow, but she didn't hear it open, so she thought she should. He was standing there with his hand on the doorknob. "Do you want me to go?"

"It would probably be best."

She turned away and started sobbing. He walked up behind her and put his arms around her.

She said, "Let's go upstairs."

Afterward, he sat on the side of the bed. "We probably shouldn't have done that."

"We are grieving, Bill. It was natural for us to come together in our grief."

He stood up and reached for his pants, which he had dropped at the side of the bed. He pulled up his underwear and uniform pants. After he did that, he turned around and said, "I'm glad you are comforting me, Gloria. Please don't do anything you will regret."

He finished dressing and left. She took a shower and scrubbed her body very hard. Her tears began and were washed away only by her thoughts of how wonderful they were in bed.

She redressed and went about her day. She was surprised that she didn't really feel bad about what she had done, which startled her.

That night, she initiated sex with John. She knew she was between her periods, and Bill hadn't used protection. She wanted to protect herself just in case she could have become pregnant. The thought made her glow.

****

A few days passed with no word from Bill. She knew she had sinned by cheating on her husband, but the biggest problem was that she didn't feel guilty and looked forward to hearing from Bill again.

A week to the day when she first comforted Bill, he called that morning to see if he could come by. She told him it would be fine. She still had her lingerie on from the night before and was putting on some makeup. The doorbell rang, and she almost tripped on the stairs running to answer it. He slipped inside and noticed her attire.

"Wow, is that just for me?"

"It could be, if you want it."

The inference was there. He put his arms around her waist and kissed her. He reached down and put his right hand inside her robe and on top of her left breast. He pressed himself toward her, and she felt his erection. She turned, and he followed her up the stairs.

He was even a better lover this time than he had been the last.

"I think if we're going to keep this up, we should meet somewhere else, Bill. I'm getting nervous about neighbors and John coming home unexpectedly."

"I agree. I'll find a place for us to meet and call you."

He called the following day and told her there was a small motel on the highway, just south of Eldridge. She told him she knew where it was and would meet him. They agreed on the following Monday. He would get the room, and she would wait in the parking lot, watching to see which room he went into, then go directly to that room.

They met there once a week for another month. During one of those weeks, John attended a four-day convention in Boston. They arranged to meet every day while he was gone. During that time, they failed to use protection. Although she was on the pill, it still made her nervous.

After John returned from his trip, she made sure they made love just in case she had become pregnant. John seemed to be oblivious to her need for so much sex. Their entire marriage, she had never initiated sex as much as she had in the last couple of months. He didn't complain, though. She and Bill continued to meet weekly for another month. After a particularly long lovemaking session, Gloria told him she was going to call it off. "We are taking a big chance, Bill. I am married, and I intend to stay that way. I'm sorry. I love you, and I have certainly enjoyed being with you."

"And I you. I understand, it is risky. You have a great life, Gloria. John is a great guy, and I feel guilty, but not for the same reasons."

"Just curious, Bill. Are you seeing anyone else?" she asked.

He wondered if she would catch on to it. "To be honest, yes, I am."

"I thought so. You are a man with needs, and I cannot fulfill them. I hope you find someone you deserve and who will be as wonderful as Geri was."

They kissed before they left the motel. She had a little regret, but after soul-searching, she realized she loved her husband and children too much and never wanted to be without them. She was also beginning to feel like a harlot, and she didn't like the feeling.

As usual, she made love with John that night. Even though Bill had used protection, there was always a chance that something might have happened. Better to be safe than sorry.

CHAPTER 39

Ally was cautiously optimistic about meeting Bill Fitzgerald. She had received her mother's blessing, but Ally could hear the concern in her voice when she said she wanted to meet him. There wasn't anything she could say that would change her mind, so it didn't really matter.

Neal took her to the airport for her nine o'clock flight to Boston. From there, she was going to rent a car and drive to Canton. Bill had given her directions, but she would depend on the GPS on her phone. She had picked out some pictures of herself as a baby. Her mother gave them to her the last time she was down there, probably because she knew she would be looking for her birth father.

She also took along a small gift. It was a decorative shell she picked up at one of the festivals. It had sea turtles on it. She thought he would like it. She guessed he was probably a fisherman, since he lived so close to the ocean.

Neal wanted to go with her, but she discouraged it, feeling she needed to face this situation alone. She didn't want any distractions. "Maybe another time," she told him, and he seemed satisfied.

The flight was a little scary because of a thunderstorm over Washington, D.C. The pilot veered around it, but they still got a few bumps. She had a toddler in the seat behind her, and the toddler was crying for almost the entire trip. Ally knew it wasn't the mom's fault; in fact, she felt sorry for her. By the time the captain announced they would be landing soon, the little girl had fallen asleep. Great timing.

The rental car was ready, and she was upgraded from a compact to an SUV. It was a Chevy Equinox, and it was very comfortable. Her GPS indicated she would arrive in Canton in an hour. She had eaten a snack on the plane and didn't feel hungry. Even though it was now after noon, she thought Bill might have some lunch planned, and she didn't want to be without an appetite.

Traffic was surprisingly light, probably because she was in between rush hours. She made good time and arrived at his driveway at one-fifteen. It was a medium-sized home for the neighborhood—a ranch style with a garage and a large front porch. There were two black rockers on the porch, with stylish black striped pillows. The yard was well-maintained, featuring a flower garden near the front door and planters on the porch ledge. She was glad he seemed to care about the look of his home.

He opened the door, apparently having heard her car. A golden retriever ran out ahead of him. It was a beautiful dog and very friendly. It ran up to her, wanting to be petted. She didn't jump on her, so she thought it was well-trained. She looked up and, for the first time, saw her father. He was a tall man with gray hair, dark brows, and hazel eyes. He was large but in a good way. Apparently, he worked out, she thought.

She held out her hand, but then he hugged her.

"I am so glad to meet you," he told her.

"Me too, you," she felt tears brim up in her eyes. She wished she had a tissue in her jacket pocket.

"How was your trip?" he asked her.

"To be expected, bumpy with a scared toddler crying behind me. Other than that, it was fine."

He laughed. "Let's go in. I'll come get your bags later."

"Oh, I wasn't planning on staying with you. I made a reservation in town."

"I might change your mind, come on."

She followed him inside, and the dog, Molly, as he called her, followed them.

"Beautiful home, Bill."

"Thank you. I try to keep it up. Now that I'm retired, I usually have one or two projects going at any given time. I have started stripping the deck paint. It is going very slowly."

Ally laughed. "That's how projects go, unfortunately."

"Tell me about yourself, Ally. I'm interested in everything."

For the next hour, Ally told him about attending college to become a nurse and her career in New York City. She also told him about losing her job during COVID because she didn't take the vaccine. They discussed how the pandemic had wreaked havoc worldwide. She learned that he volunteered during the COVID-19 pandemic at the local hospital, where he worked in security.

"I enjoyed it. At least I could get out every day. Even if I had to wear a mask," he told her.

Ally continued, "I found a job in North Carolina doing catering. It's something I would have never seen myself doing, but I think circumstances change, and you change with them or get left behind."

"Tell me about your mother. We haven't kept in touch. After losing Geri, I remarried and moved to Ohio for a while. The marriage didn't work out, and I felt Aaron needed family around, so we moved back here about a year after we had moved to Ohio. It was an adjustment. Fortunately, I was able to get my old job back, and we were okay."

"So, you never remarried?"

"No, I didn't. Never found anyone to settle down with. Maybe it was me. Where are your parents now?"

"My parents retired and moved to Bartow, Florida. Mother had an aunt who lived there years ago, and she convinced my father to move there."

Ally wondered if it bothered Bill when she mentioned her father; after all, he was the only father she knew. She didn't see him react, so she didn't press it.

"So they stay busy?"

"They did up until a couple of years ago. That's when my father started showing signs of dementia. They were still busy, but over the last six months, everything has come to a halt. I'm not sure if I mentioned it or not, but my sister's daughter was killed in an auto accident earlier this year."

"I'm so sorry, no, I didn't know that. How did that happen?"

"She and her boyfriend were going up a mountain road in Western North Carolina and came across a boulder in the middle of the road. It's a wonder it didn't fall on them. Anyway, while trying to turn around, we think they hit the guardrail, which had been damaged by the severe hurricane that had come through the previous year. When it gave way, their car went flying off into a gorge. It was buried under dense brush, and the authorities took a while to find the wreckage. We were told they would have been killed instantly."

"That's terrible. Is that Janet's daughter?"

"Yes, that's right. I guess you knew my brother and sister."

"I knew Craig better, since he and Aaron were friends."

"Did you know about me?" asked Ally.

"I wish I had, Ally. We moved away probably while your mom was pregnant with you. She never contacted me once we stopped seeing each other, so I had no idea she was pregnant. She, of course, was still with your father, so there was just as much a possibility of you being his flesh and blood. Does it bother you?"

"What do you think?" she stared at him.

He had to look away, and when he looked back, she could see tears in his eyes. "I guess you have a lot of anger about finding out."

"You know, I had not thought of it as anger. I guess I have been in such shock that it hasn't occurred to me that I should be angry."

"That's understandable."

"What good would it do for me to be angry? It wouldn't change anything. You were only the sperm donor."

"That is true. John was the fortunate fellow who raised you, and I can see he did a good job. I hope you will accept me as a friend, or at least as an acquaintance. I don't deserve to be called father."

At that moment, all of the pent-up emotions she had been holding back, from losing Rachel to finding out she was not her father's child, hit her like a brick. She started sobbing. Not for the years lost from her birth father, but for the lack of knowing who she was and where she belonged in the order of the universe. She took the tissue Bill handed her and dried her eyes.

"I'm sorry. I didn't think I would be this emotional. My husband, Neal, wanted to come, but I discouraged him. I wanted us to meet alone. I don't have any feelings toward you, good or bad, Bill. I'm a grown woman who just had her world turned upside down in the span of a few months. I hope you will give me time to get used to my new normal."

"I definitely will. I'm so sorry we had to meet under these circumstances. It's funny, I thought you would look a little like me, but you look like your mother, who, by the way, was a beautiful woman."

"Yes, she is."

"Let's go on the front porch. I have made a few sandwiches and prepared some lemonade. Does that sound good?"

"It sure does. I am getting hungry."

"Tonight, I'm going to take you to one of the best restaurants in Canton, and you can have all the lobster you can eat."

"That sounds great, Bill."

CHAPTER 40

Over the next two days, Bill showed Ally Boston. They went to a baseball game, and he took her to Fanuel Hall. She visited Harvard University and attended a Boston Pops concert.

His son, Aaron, flew in the day after she arrived, and they got to know each other over beers at Bill's favorite bar. Aaron attended Northwestern, earning a degree in civil engineering and a master's in mathematics. He currently teaches math at Miami University in Ohio and also has his own engineering firm. She learned he had married an OBGYN, and they have three children, including twins.

"You have your hands full," she told him.

"We do, but I love it. My in-laws live nearby and are a big help with the kids."

"Ya'll are welcome to come see me anytime. I live on a beautiful beach in coastal North Carolina."

"We will, thank you."

"Do I detect a Southern accent?" asked Bill.

Ally laughed, "Yes, I did pick it up, ya'll. By the way, you're invited, too."

"Thank you, Ally. I would love to spend time with you, especially in the winter."

"We do have better weather in the winter than Boston, but it can get chilly. Try to come in the late Spring or early Summer."

The time went by fast, and it was her time to fly back home. She was missing Neal and Lucky. She had stayed at the Inn in town, insisting she would be more comfortable doing that. Bill seemed deflated, but once Aaron arrived, he was busy with him at home.

On their last night together, Ally pulled out the baby pictures her mom had given her and showed them to Bill. He enjoyed looking at them and commented on how cute she was. She had seen pictures of Geri, even one with her and her mom in their tennis outfits. Bill pointed it out. "Those gals loved their tennis."

They agreed to stay in touch by email, and perhaps she and Neal would fly up the following summer.

Neal was at the airport when she arrived. She texted him when she got through baggage claim. He hugged her tight and told her how much he missed her.

"You might just get lucky tonight if you keep this up," she teased him. "Speaking of Lucky, how's my boy?"

"Fat and happy."

"He'd better not be fat. What have you been feeding him?"

"Just teasing, he's fine. Eating his regular portion of food."

On the drive home, she called Mary to see if she wanted to go to the gym the next day. Mary said yes and said she would pick her up at nine o'clock. "Bring your swimsuit," she told her.

Then she called Three Island Catering. Gene answered, rather than Sarah.

"Hello Gene. How are you? I'm calling to see if any jobs are coming up?"

He said, "Oh, Ally, we are worried about Sarah."

"What do you mean?"

"She's missing. I haven't heard from her for two days."

"Missing? What?"

"I'm at a loss. Can you help out at the office?"

"Absolutely", said Ally. "I'll be there in an hour. Do you have any idea of what could have happened to her?"

"I have a bad feeling. She started signing up on some dating sites. She was cautious, hard to please."

"So, you think it might have something to do with those?"

"I don't know, it's just a hunch. She's very private, as you know. After you get here, I'll go out to her house."

"I don't want you to go alone. Why don't I bring Neal? Safety in numbers. I'm not saying you're in any danger, but this sounds serious. Sarah has never been out of the office, unless she was sick."

"Okay, see if he can come. I don't know what I will be walking into."

Neal agreed to go with her to help Gene. He knew Ally would get involved, and he was concerned about her safety. Ally called Mary and cancelled their gym plans for the next few days, but hesitated in telling her why. She just told her she had forgotten about a dental appointment. She will get Mary involved if anything untoward arises. They make a great team in solving mysteries. Mary would be champing at the bit if she told her anything now.

When they arrived, Ally sensed how nervous and upset Gene was, and she did her best to comfort him. "She probably doesn't feel well, and maybe she thought she called you. It will be okay."

Gene brought her up to date on everything that was on the books, in case she received any calls. They were booked for two weeks.

"You may be able to fit in a small function on Wednesday. That is our slowest day."

"I know, I'll be fine," she reassured him. They left a few minutes later for Sarah's house, and Ally said a prayer.

ABOUT THE AUTHOR

I retired from nursing in 2016. In 2020, I developed an autoimmune syndrome called 'Burning Mouth'. It is precisely what it sounds like-a very painful burn constantly in the mouth. Through trial and error, I found a medication regimen that helped, and, more importantly, a doctor willing to help me.

A lifelong reader and a true crime junkie, I combined these passions and began writing. Creativity is an incredible healer. It helped me during the worst time of discovering a plan of care for my syndrome.

Missing people is my primary interest, and I follow podcasts which delve into subjects of disappearances.

Previous books include:

A Measure of Kindness
A Lie More Real Than Truth (based on a real event)
Saving Lisa

Kindly leave a review on Amazon or Goodreads. It would be most appreciated!

Sincerely,

E. L. Boyer

www.ingramcontent.com/pod-product-compliance
Lightning Source LLC
Chambersburg PA
CBHW051957220626
47052CB00004B/988